Jeanile's arms slowly traveled delightfully up Ravenell's strong arms to rest gently around his neck as she tiled her head back and closed her eyes in anticipation of the sweet sensation of kissing him. This was not a kiss to be taken lightly, nor was it a kiss that was given in the heat of the moment. It was a kiss that simply said hello and thank you for being you....

Wylde Honey

A *Siren* Production of

Wylde Honey

Cover Illustration
Cover Art & Graphic Design by:
Justin Walker of
justinwalkero@yahoo.com

Editor: Kevin Mills
www.paperpolisher.com

Note for Librarians: A cataloguing record for this book is available from Library and Archives
Canada at www.collectionscanada.ca/amicus/index-e.html
ISBN 1-4120-8371-0

*Trafford's print shop runs on "green energy" from solar, wind and other environmentally-friendly
power sources.*

TRAFFORD
PUBLISHING™

Offices in Canada, USA, Ireland and UK
This book was published *on-demand* in cooperation with Trafford Publishing. On-demand
publishing is a unique process and service of making a book available for retail sale to the
public taking advantage of on-demand manufacturing and Internet marketing. On-demand
publishing includes promotions, retail sales, manufacturing, order fulfilment, accounting and
collecting royalties on behalf of the author.

Book sales for North America and international:
Trafford Publishing, 6E–2333 Government St.,
Victoria, BC V8T 4P4 CANADA
phone 250 383 6864 (toll-free 1 888 232 4444)
fax 250 383 6804; email to orders@trafford.com
Book sales in Europe:
Trafford Publishing (UK) Limited, 9 Park End Street, 2nd Floor
Oxford, UK OX1 1HH UNITED KINGDOM
phone 44 (0)1865 722 113 (local rate 0845 230 9601)
facsimile 44 (0)1865 722 868; info.uk@trafford.com
Order online at:
trafford.com/06-0126

10 9 8 7 6 5 4 3 2

Dedicated to
LUVROSE, OHMELLO, WOODEN, BIGBOOTY P.,
Daphne "Hustla" Robinson
Brenda & Larry Leighton
&
Robin "Sugar Lips" Sherman
With all my love and thanks.

Extra special thanks to:
Kevin "the God of Editing" Mills
The talented Justin Walker
Noel "my shorty in the cargo pants" Rivera
Kathie Baiardi, Jean Rodriquez & Melanie Ravenell
Angela Apostalakas
Beth "Beffie" Cunningham & Morgan Brown
Lou "Knight in Shinning Armor" Epstein
The lovely Ladies of Delta Phi Epsilon (Beta Omega)
Richard M. Betheil, Esq.
St. John's University
Arold Placide
&
My Latina Sister, Deliana Pagan

FOR

Matthew Tristan Leonard

Passion For Sex

You warned you'd run at first
Mention of commitment.
Your insatiable thirst--
Sexually intimate--
Poured out parameters.
Otherwise, a spirit free:
Generous encounters
That welcome ecstasy.
Not sure why you'd said this;
I pondered your concern
For entertaining bliss
That's not to be cornered.
       Similar sentiments have I...
       Let us go now, between your thighs!

By Scott Hastings for his beloved Goddess Feb. '05

Wylde Honey

By

Shamaine Diana Henry

PROLOGUE

One foot in front of the other! That's all you have to do. It's okay... he won't notice you. It would be too painful....

As her eyes devoured Ravenell from across the room, panic coursed through her body like an electric current, keeping her feet anchored firmly to the ground, paralyzed. Praying that he wouldn't turn around helped Jeanile ignore the beads of sweat that made her palms slippery, almost to the point where she desperately needed to put down her suitcase and create some distance between them.

Several people in line boarding Flight 780 to *Costa Del Sol* turned around to stare at the noise caused by Jeanile's suitcase as it fell to the tile floor with a thud. Ravenell's eyes met hers in a brief glance of recognition. His warm, sherry-colored eyes locked with hers and immediately the bottom of her stomach fell out at the unmistakable anger seething in his eyes at the sight of her. Before she had a moment to react, his anger vanished, replaced instead by the cool, unshakable look of someone who had finally caught the rat that had been eating his cheese.

Unable to hold his stare, Jeanile looked around frantically for any means of escape. There was none. The *Making Peace with Your Sensuality* convention awaited her in Spain and she realized there was absolutely no excuse she could offer them because she was, after all, their keynote speaker. She tried to rationalize that her cold, clammy hands and her irregular breathing was only due to the stress of the situation. In the back of her mind, she wondered what her patients would think of such a cowardly reaction. It definitely wasn't the fact that the sight of him brought back the heat of those long summer nights, nights where the stars would dance in the heavens and the breeze would caress their naked bodies as she snuggled closer and closer to her lover's heartbeat. The long, steamy summer nights when Ravenell would hold her in his arms, nibble on her neck as the unrelenting heat from his body would melt into hers....

Ravenell turned around without so much of an eyebrow raised in response to the stricken look sketched across her face.

Jeanile picked up her suitcase and tried to ignore the disappointment that began to settle into the pit of her stomach. *I guess that's it. No fireworks.*

No small talk. Only the expected anger and maybe a little hatred. She frowned. *Well, I could hate him too, I guess... but I don't. So many memories and so many regrets, but it's too late to change the past.*

The line moved forward and life went on.

"Miss...? Your ticket, please?" The flight attendant interrupted her inner monologue.

Jeanile absentmindedly handed it to her, returning to her thoughts. How many times had she picked up the telephone to call him, to explain herself, only to return the headset to its cradle, consumed with defeat? There was too much hurt - said and unsaid - between them. And now? Now not even a spark of recognition. As if nothing had ever happened. Obviously Ravenell had moved on.

"Thank you, and enjoy your flight." The flight attendant smiled as she handed back the boarding pass and motioned her towards the plane.

Struggling with her suitcase, Jeanile made her way through the boarding tunnel, toward the plane and finally saw her seat row. She froze. Dread hit her like an unbearable wave as the sight of Ravenell relaxing comfortably in his seat came into view. There was an empty window seat next to him, and Jeanile prayed that she wouldn't have to sit through a six-and-a-half hour flight next to the man who once could have been her husband. Every step she took brought her that much closer to him. The panic she had experienced earlier again washed over her as her feet and the suitcase became heavier and heavier.

"Here, let me help you." His deep, controlled voice unexpectedly split the air. Jeanile's heart momentarily stopped at the sound.

She watched in fascination as Ravenell gently took the suitcase from her numb fingers and stored it in the overhead compartment. Nervously, she looked at the number on her ticket and back at the number printed above his seat. To her surprise and slight relief, they didn't match. Looking over him, she located her seat in the window seat directly behind his. Silently, she slid into her seat and prepared herself for the Flight from Hell, where she would have to sit mere inches away from the man whom she had left standing at the alter four years ago....

UNO

It had been an uncommonly cool night for July. It was the first Friday night that it hadn't rained in the last two months, and it seemed as if everyone had come to Club Envy to get rid of their cabin fever. The men came out in droves to admire the scantily clad women and enjoy the popular DJ Ron Don spin his magic on the turntables. The lights were dimmed, the music was loud and everyone was just out to have a great time.

Toward the center of the upper level, four very stunning women sat in a booth, casually surveying the dance floor below them.

For a petite woman, Ramika was easily the leader of the pack because of her frank nature and a take-charge attitude. She was always impeccably dressed. She knew how to get her point across, whether through words or her very honed and skillful use of body language. If there was a party, community service, luncheon or shopping expedition that was worthwhile, Ramika, had her hand in it. Tonight she had dragged Jeanile out of her self-made prison. She was going to get her to party and enjoy herself, even if it killed the both of them! Her neatly waxed eyebrows were raised in disdain at a few of the crappy-looking men who should have been turned away at the door hours ago.

Tracya had both looks and brains, but for some reason she always underestimated her worth. Her long, silky auburn hair was flipped provocatively over her left ear to show off one of her best features - her very good taste in jewelry. Her leather-clad feet tapped distractedly in time to the music, as she wondered how she would get through a dance without popping out of the top Ramika had convinced her to squeeze her ample chest in. Ramika had taken the shy little Southerner under her very experienced and capable wings on Tracya's first day on campus. She never regretted that day. They were fast friends, able to see eye to eye on almost all issues of importance. The fact that Ramika did most of the leading while Tracya followed quietly along didn't seem to bother anyone, either.

Dominique, on the other hand, was not easily led around by anyone. She had her own opinions and wasn't afraid to make them known. The gentle tug-of-war that went on between Dominique and Ramika kept the group lively and on their toes. With her short-cropped hair, kind dark eyes and large, brilliant smile, she always knew just how far to push Ramika before things got out of hand.

Tonight, the usual friendly fire was put on the back burner because they had come out to party and help Jeanile rise out of her doldrums. Three pairs of eyes watched tentatively as Jeanile slowly sipped her favorite drink, balefully surveying the club with a disinterested eye.

"Girl, it's about time you took us up on our offer to get you out of that dorm room. Look at all the fine-looking brothers out there, just *waiting* to be reformed." Ramika waved a well-manicured hand at the wide expanse of the dance floor of Club Envy.

Jeanile shook her head. "Been there, done that," she said in a jaded voice.

"Hey, don't let Gary cheat you out of a good time." Ramika warned her. "For my part, I never let *any* man rob me of my sense of fun."

"Amen to that, my sister!" Tracya took a deep refreshing swallow from her *Screaming Orgasm* as she eyed the dance floor looking for a suitable partner — dance or otherwise.

"What you need is another drink to put you in the right frame of mind," Tracya offered kindly.

Dominique gently placed a soothing hand on Jeanile's shoulder, as if to say *"don't let these fools drag you into anything too soon."* Out of the four women, Jeanile was the only one with her head set firmly on her shoulders. She didn't play games. She wasn't about to take crap from any man, but she knew all too well that even bigger mistakes were made when one was on the rebound from a recent and painful breakup.

"The last thing I will ever do is to let a cheating, no good, two-timing bastard like Gary get under my skin. And I'll be *damned* if I let him drive me to drink!" Jeanile eyed the *Screaming Orgasm* that Tracya ordered for her without enthusiasm.

"Oh, cut the drama," Ramika intoned. "It's not like we're sending you on a binge-drinking expedition! I swear, sometime you just overreact." A muscle in Ramika's jaw clenched unconsciously.

"I guess I can be a bit of a drama queen, at times," Jeanile conceded sheepishly.

"At times?" All three of her friends chorused in disbelief.

"After all," Jeanile continued while trying to ignore their incredulous stares, "It's been a little over eight months…" Her voice stalled a bit and her bravado slipped as the memory of him flooded her mind. The man who had broken her heart by sleeping with her best friend.

"Are you still counting?!?" Ramika cut off her train of thought. She could see that Jeanile was about to slip back into her land of self-depreciation. She really didn't want to hear how in love Jeanile was. Ramika was sick and tired of the self-pity Jeanile tended to wallow in, and all because her man had cheated on her. It was time to move on, and it was going to be tonight or never. Having witnessed the entire drama, Ramika was not going to let Jeanile re-live it — at least not in public.

Gary and Jeanile had met on Campus. It had been natural for them to fall into a steady pattern that turned into a friendship that turned into a romance. With every conversation they shared, they seemed to have more and more in common. The only problem was that Gary was a horny toad, and Jeanile was naive and headstrong. Raised to believe that love and marriage went hand in hand, she wasn't about to go against the grain of her parents' teachings.

To be honest, Ramika had always been a bit envious of Jeanile's blinding trust in love. A love she had longed for, but had given up on the idea a long time ago. She was the author of her fate, and she was definitely *not* going to put her future into any man's hands. She was particularly glad — privately, of course — when Jeanile had come running to her with tears in her eyes and a broken heart in her hands. Her faith in the self-centeredness of men had been restored, and she had stalwartly inflicted her own brand of justice on Gary.

It was the least Ramika could do for a "good friend" who had just opened the door of her boyfriend's apartment to glimpse ass and other unmentionable body parts in motion — complete with the animalistic soundtrack that filled their apartment. Gary had had the nerve to have another woman! In their bed! Now Ramika had taken Jeanile under her wings. She would make it her business to teach Jeanile a thing or two about control and how to keep men guessing. That was eight months ago. Despite all of her attempts, Jeanile had not proven herself an apt pupil. Jeanile had simply not been able to move on.

"Of course she's not counting. She's been too busy with her course work and her thesis. Being an intern in the psychology department isn't a piece of cake. Besides, she hasn't taken a break from her last degree to this one. Behaving like an academic superwoman would wear anyone out," Dominique defended. She shook her head. There were times when she could swear that Ramika had a hidden agenda.

"Being an English major isn't exactly a piece of cake, either, you know."

"Ramika, I didn't say that it was, but try diving through a bunch of Freudian theories some day..."

"Is that the one that ties sex, repression and incest into a neat little bundle?" Ramika asked innocently, her eyes following the cute bartender around.

"Oh, please. Stick to Shakespeare and Langston Hughes. Freud is a little over your head," Dominique said with a wry smile.

"Fine, it doesn't matter what it's about or whether or not she's missing the bastard. Fact of the matter is this place is jumping, and we're gonna be the life of the party. It's just a few minutes after one and we have plenty of time to do some damage, ladies. And just in case some of you need an incentive, I'll bet good money with Jeanile that she can't get that guy over here and his number in her pocket."

Four pairs of eyes looked toward the bar area where a bunch of guys were lounging and watching the dance floor greedily.

"Oh, sweetie. Not the guy in the brown shirt blinding every girl that passes by him with his wannabe platinum jewelry?" Tracya asked in disgust. "Please..."

"Of course not. I picked a challenge, not a desperation." Ramika flashed her a look to tell her she should have known better.

"Ohm! The one that didn't give you the time of day the last time you were in here?" Tracya asked and swallowed a groan as Ramika stepped on her toes, a word or two too late.

"He's yummy!" Jeanile whispered.

"Girl, I don't think anyone says 'yummy' anymore," Tracya informed her.

"And when have you known me to care what the word of the year is?"

"Just trying to help," Tracya apologized half-heartedly.

Ramika decided to head off the impending storm that was brewing between Tracya and Jeanile. "Do you want the bet or not?" she asked.

"Yeah, I want it." Jeanile held her gaze.

"Well, what are you waiting for? Go get him." Ramika pushed her toward the edge of the booth.

"In my own time," Jeanile said, shrugging off Ramika's hand. "First, I'm going to dance." Three pairs of eyes watched eagerly as Jeanile walked over to the jumping dance floor. With her long legs and well-formed body, she turned more than a few heads. However, the side bets that were made as the crowd devoured her proved that her friends knew it was all just a brave show of courage. Notwithstanding the self-assured walk and the sensual sway of her hips, she was still a shy woman at heart. It would take a little more than courage for her to approach the fine-looking brother who was enjoying himself at the end of the bar.

Jeanile reveled on the dance floor, sending more than a few body temperatures rising to the ceiling. Cautiously eyeing her chosen target at the end of the bar, Jeanile assessed her chances of winning the bet. He was tall - very tall - and well-dressed, but unlike most of the men in the club he didn't seem interested in the women who were giving him the eye. He was talking with the bartender and the man standing to his right.

Jeanile's stomach took a nosedive when she realized that she would have an audience. After all, he was ignoring the blatant attempts made by the other ladies to get his attention. What made her think she even had a chance? The fact that he had turned Ramika down was amazing, but it also made it very possible that she would embarrass herself and leave the club without his number. Deciding against risking embarrassment in this very crowded setting, she started back towards the girls. One look at

Tracya's pleased face and Ramika's smug look of triumph stopped her in her tracks.

They are not going to get the better of me! She thought as she stiffened her spine and prepared for the worst. She turned around and walked toward the bar.

"Excuse me."

Ravenell Wylde turned around to stare down at the very beautiful Nubian sister who was trying to tell him something over the beat of the blazing speakers surrounding the dance floor of Club Envy.

"Yes?" Fixing a pleasant smile on his lips, not quite believing his luck. His eyes discreetly skimmed her figure, marveled that such a compact figure came with some equally delightful curves. She wore limited make up, and from the style of her hair he could tell that she wasn't one to wear a weave — at least not tonight.

Ravenell leaned a little closer to her to hear what she was saying over the pounding bass of the speakers. He was pleasantly surprised by the slightly elusive scent of her perfume. He tried to concentrate on what she was saying, despite the very attractive motion of her chest.

"My friends and I were staring at you from across the room," pointing in the general direction of three other fine-looking ladies. "And we wanted to know if we could buy you a drink?"

"All four of you?" His smile widened as she looked guiltily away. "If I didn't know better, I would think that you were blushing." He delighted in the fact that she squirmed even more.

"Well..." She took a deep breath to steady herself, the form-fitting cream tank top that she wore emphasizing her breasts as she inhaled. Ravenell noticed and swiftly brought his eyes back to hers before the heat that was generating in the pit of his stomach spread to more telltale areas. "We wanted to reward you for being the only gentleman in the club. We've watched men grab, manhandle and approach us with the weakest of lines and we have to say that you're a gentleman because you haven't grabbed anyone... yet. Fortunately, the time limit we placed on the experiment has run out and you're the lucky winner."

"Are you serious?" He gaped as the flood of her words came to a halt. She was a challenge of contradictions. She admitted to watching him and other guys in the club, she degraded him by putting a price and even a doubt on his intentions and she had the nerve to try him, judge him and now reward him without even so much as a by-your-leave. She had completely turned the tables, and he found that although he was unprepared for this occurrence, he was at least extremely intrigued.

"I'm absolutely serious," Jeanile said. "Oh, maybe I should introduce myself. I'm Jeanile Graham, and the ladies drooling over there are Ramika Jackson, Tracya Eden and Dominique Allen." *Crud. Maybe I shouldn't have given him my full name. Or theirs! I must look and sound like a fool.*

"Ravenell Wylde."

The electricity that shot up his arm as his hand swallowed her palm in a handshake stole the words from his mouth. They stood there staring at each other for a few seconds.

"Well?" Jeanile asked as she slowly and reluctantly took her hand from his.

"Well, what?" Ravenell asked blankly. *I really must seem like the village idiot at this point,* he thought to himself.

"What would you like to drink?" She pronounced the words slowly, exaggerating every word to make sure that he would be able to read her lips. But the sensual movement of her lips distracted him, and lengthy seconds crept by before Ravenell was able to give her a coherent answer.

"Corona's fine, thanks." Accepting the drink from the bartender and giving the rest of the males surrounding the bar a furtive look, he watched sheepishly as Jeanile paid the bartender. Fascinated eyes watched as her long, shapely legs carried her gracefully through the gyrating crowd toward her friends. The muscles in her body mesmerized him in such a way that he almost trampled her when she came to a sudden halt.

Jeanile flipped her long, silky hair over her right shoulder as she gave him a reassuring smile.

*   *   *

The sun beamed bright and cheery as Jeanile jogged her fourth lap around the man-made pond at Eisenhower Park. It had not promised to be a glorious day, but she had been determined to stick with her plan. She was going to eat right, exercise more and be good to herself. If she couldn't love herself - inside and out - then she couldn't expect anyone else to. Dominque had decided to bury herself in the self-help isle of her favorite bookstores, Tracya had a steady relationship and Ramika was happy with controlling her Mr. Right Now, which she had picked up at a recent party. Jeanile, on the other hand, had spent the last two weeks reflecting on the relationship patterns that littered her past. Every single one of the guys she dated was a particular type, she realized. They were successful, ambitious and sincere. At least, they were sincere in the beginning. Eventually, however, they had all cheated on her. She tried to improve and become more independent than ever — outwardly — but deep inside there was the fear that any man she would give her heart to will eventually step out to greener pastures. Just like everyone else had.

Jeanile sighed deeply and frowned. She was determined to break the cycle and be on her own, for as long as it took. She wanted to make sure that she was strong enough to take on whatever awaited her on the love horizon. The fact was that the image of Ravenell, the very handsome brother she had all but picked up at Club Envy a few weeks ago continued to haunt her thoughts, yet simultaneously strengthened her resolve. She would probably regret for months that she hadn't given him her telephone number.

She jogged in place to the soothing sounds of the early morning park life. A family of ducks was frolicking in the pond, there were other joggers sharing the path and a group of very rowdy men were on the lawn ahead of her playing Sunday morning football. Straightening her jogging suit, she continued on the path, only to stop suddenly when a football hit her hard on the lower part of her thigh. Rubbing the sore spot, Jeanile looked around for the culprit only to be confronted by a group of very contrite-looking, overgrown boys.

"Sorry, Miss," number thirteen apologized as he came down the path to retrieve the ball.

"Not a problem," Jeanile replied, but was distracted by the very tall and very real Ravenell Wylde as he came to investigate what was holding up the game.

"Oh... uhm... hello," Ravenell greeted her as he hurried the youngster back to the playing field.

"Hello."

Jeanile was a bit uncomfortable with this chance encounter. She felt the sweat build on the palms of her hands, her breath coming fast and furious as she tried to take it all in. It took all of her will power not to reach up to pat her hair, making sure all her strands were in its proper place.

"Mr. Wylde?" It seemed he was holding up the football game as the players eagerly awaited the continuation of their game.

"I'll be right there," he shouted over his shoulder.

"Listen, I'm sorry I didn't call you." *What could she possibly say? 'I took your number as a part of a bet, and then I washed the paper with your telephone number by accident?' It was the truth. I simply forgot it was in the pocket of the pants I wore that night. I'm attracted to you, but the men I'm attracted to usually end up hurting me so I couldn't call you because I am very, very attracted to you? I didn't call you but I've thought about you constantly, and regretted not giving you my telephone number? How's that for desperation?* She thought hard as she tried to add something suitable to her last and very vague sentence.

"It's okay," Ravenell said. "I'll admit, my ego was a bit bruised, but it's just as well." He smiled down at her. The Gods were really smiling on him.

"Really?" Now it was her turn to endure a bruised ego.

"Absolutely. It gives me the chance to invite you out for coffee. Or brunch, or whatever you feel comfortable doing. This way we can start again, without the distraction of loud music or the misapprehension that you're buying me a drink so that you can drag me off by my hair to your cave at the end of the night."

"Cute." The corners of Jeanile's full lips turned up in the beginning of a smile. It widened when Ravenell joined her in a brief smile.

"Mr. Wylde?" The call was even more impatient than the last one.

"I would, but I have nothing to wear." Jeanile whispered.

"Neither do I." Ravenell looked pointedly down at his gray sweat suit with grass stains on the knees and bum.

"Ah, point taken. Why don't we have coffee and cake at the *Witch's Brew* just down the road from here when your game is over?" she suggested.

"That'll be just fine. Feel free to come up and watch the end of the game if you'd like to. When you're finished jogging," he invited eagerly.

"Thanks. I think I will."

Jeanile watched as he sauntered back to the impatient group of boys. The banter and teasing she heard Ravenell endure brought a triumphant smile to her lips as she started to finish her jog around the lake.

*   *   *

The *Witches Brew* was a well-known local coffeehouse that attracted the chocolate lover and adventure-seekers alike, due to its very gothic name and delicious delights. On any given Sunday, one could see teenagers in dark gothic clothing with colorful hair next to housewives taking a much-needed break, along with the average Joes out to taste the local delights. The atmosphere was one that soothed frazzled nerves with the hypnotic, new age sounds spilling comfortably from the hidden speakers, overstuffed sofas, loveseats and armchairs strategically scattered around the dimly lit room.

"I would never have noticed this place, much less thought it was your kind of hangout," Ravenell ventured after the waitress had seated them. They sat close to a window overlooking the nicely manicured lawn that sported a huge cauldron.

"Don't let the decorations fool you. I doubt this place is actually frequented by modern day witches. But if you're really nice to me, I can introduce you to Jez and *then* you'll get an eyeful," Jeanile teased.

"Jez?" Curiosity had gotten the cat.

"It's short for Jezebel, and she could probably give you a nice tour of the *Witch's Brew*." Jeanile flashed him a mysterious smile and Ravenell found himself smiling back.

"I guess that means you come here often?"

"I love it here. I try to come here as often as my busy schedule allows." She shrugged her shoulders. "I guess it's because it's so nestled away from the hustle and bustle of your average coffeehouse. They serve everything you could possible want here except pretension. You won't find your coffee in all the various flavors or sizes. Here one size fits all. They give refills and they have the basic flavors, but what they go overboard with is the variety of chocolate. They've got everything you could conceivably add chocolate to." She smiled and looked down at the table. "I guess I sound like a walking commercial for this place, don't I?"

"Not at all. I like watching your face light up as you talk about it." *Did I really say that out loud? The guys would definitely think I've gone soft if they saw me mooning over this woman — even though she's as beautiful and as smooth as butter cream.* Clearing his thoughts, Ravenell asked her to tell him more. She beamed.

"Well, every now and then a cute fireman strolls in from the firehouse next door. So, that's always an added attraction, as well as the house specialty, which is a chocolate fudge mousse cake called *Death by Chocolate.*"

"Mmm... sounds tempting." Ravenell's eyes twinkled as he stared at her.

"The fireman?" Jeanile teased, raising an eyebrow.

"No, *Death by Chocolate.* I have a very sweet tooth." He was desperately searching his mind to find something funny to say. He yearned to hear her laugh again. On the ride back from the football game, some of the boys on his team had her laughing to the point of tears. Her smile dazzled him as he listened to them give her a blow by blow account of why they felt they lost this week's game.

"Uhm..." Jeanile glanced nervously— excitedly—around the room. Had she just gotten lost in his eyes? If that was the case, she was glad— she wasn't the only one staring. She searched her mind, but the only thing she could come up with was.... "Your kids seem to adore you."

"Kids?"

Ravenell had to blink to catch up to the conversation. "Oh.... You mean my Terror Squad."

Jeanile nodded her head as she buried her eyes in the decadent menu with its chocolate cakes, ice creams and sundaes. Delightful ways to utilize every last item on the menu kept her from meeting his eyes.

"They're a great bunch. They're just starving for attention."

"So how long have you been teaching?" Jeanile picked a neutral topic to try and keep things on an even keel.

"Teaching?" he asked. "Actually, I don't teach. Well, not in the classroom, at least. I just volunteer my time and I ended up coaching this team. To be honest, I kind of got this bunch by default, but I'm enjoying every moment of it."

"You do this every Sunday?" Jeanile had to admit that the fact that he was doing something altruistic only enhanced his attractive personality.

"Throughout the football season, which starts in about three weeks. This was just a scrimmage. Things won't heat up until well into September. It keeps the kids off the streets and motivated."

"It's rare to see a brother giving back to the community, you know." Jeanile couldn't keep the admiration from her voice.

"I'm not giving back that much. Just a few hours on a Sunday morning, really. Besides, I'm sure there are a lot of other men out there doing so much more than I do."

"You're too generous. And modest, to boot."

"Notice, I said 'men' and not 'boys,'" Ravenell clarified. He hoped that she wasn't one of those men bashers. Sisters need to realize that men carried around as much baggage as women do. All they had to contend with are things they let their men get away with. Men, on the other hand, had to look out for skanks, gold-diggers and fakers. When the real thing comes along, it's usually mistaken for something else entirely because of all the games women played.

"True, but sometimes the distinction is hard to make. Men will usually say and do most anything to get what they want."

"And women won't?" His left eyebrow was raised to emphasize his question.

"Yes, but it's not like the games guys play. C'mon, you know guys are just after one thing."

He shook his head. "Not all the time. Sometimes, sure, because of the bait women set out with hopes of getting a platinum ring. It confuses things. You might go home with your dream woman and wake up to a nightmare."

Jeanile preoccupied herself with making sure that the waitress handed her the *Death by Chocolate* while Ravenell received the *Chocolate Caramel Mousse*.

"Come on, this is too heavy a topic to discuss over chocolate. Tell me something about you. What do you do for work and pleasure?" He wanted to hear all about her.

"I'm still in Grad-school, but I'm interning at Creedmoor."

"The nut house?" Disbelief seeped into Ravenell's voice.

"Yes, the *mental institution.*" She placed particular emphasis on her last two words. "By the time I'm finished with my studies, I'll be a certified... sex therapist."

Ravenell almost choked on his bite of creamy mousse.

"Are you alright?" Jeanile asked with a mischievous smile on her lips. She had deliberately said it to get a reaction out of him.

"Yeah. I think so, I just bit off a little more than I can chew and it went down the wrong hole." Ravenell coughed and reached for his water, trying to regain his equilibrium.

"Funny, I've heard similar statements quite a few times from different patients."

Ravenell smiled at her deliberate misrepresentation of his words. "With a little imagination and lack of oxygen, I could almost believe that you said 'sex therapist.'" He continued.

"I did."

His dark brown eyes searched her mellow golden ones. Of all the occupations out there, he would never have pegged for her being a Dr. Ruth. "Are you serious?"

"Sure I am."

He paused, smiling. "So… what's it like?"

Jeanile flushed. "Like any other profession, I suppose. Except we really mean it when we say that we're passionate about our job."

His laugh was deep and sensual, playing on her hormones like Tito Puente and his amazing drums. The color of his eyes lightened to a rich brown, and the sides of his eyes crinkled with delight as his amused lips parted to flash a glimpse of perfect, white teeth. Jeanile responded to his smile with a curve of her lips and a hurried crossing of her legs. *Is he aware of the havoc he's creating with the very depth of his voice?* She wondered as the moment passed and her heartbeat went back to normal.

"So tell me," he said, "what led you to want to be a sex therapist?" The smirk that tilted the corners of her mouth implied that there was a tantalizing story at the end of her smile. It would take a lot more than chocolate and a smile to wheedle it out of her. He spent the next couple of hours trying to get her to divulge the story, only to be rewarded with her telephone number and the promise of another date…

DOS

The sight of the sun-drenched steps of the Metropolitan Museum of Art were aged a lovely color of coconut cream, bringing a becoming smile to Jeanile's face. A thrill went down her spine to settle in the pit of her stomach as Ravenell casually slipped his hand around her waist. They fell into an easy gait as they mounted the steps side by side.

"Art?" Ravenell asked, his left eyebrow lifting skeptically. "When I wheedled another date out of you, I didn't think I would be dragged to... well... a..."

"...a place filled with some of the most priceless works of art?" She inquired, glancing up at him with a smile.

"Technically, but you're the first woman to invite me here for a date! Besides, I would think a sex therapist would take me to the museum of sex or something."

"Afraid not. I rarely take my work home with me. Analyzing someone's sexual map and walking through an exhibit on sex in all its various forms - deviant and otherwise - is not my idea of a first date."

"*Second* date," he said.

She grinned at him, but in the back of her mind she questioned if he was teasing her about it being a second date, or if he was really as petulant as he sounded.

Ravenell flashed her a huge smile as he gave her the gentle reminder. The wink he gave her convinced her that he was, in fact, only messing with her head. They shared a smile for a few more seconds, and just like that, the day took on a lighthearted feel that rivaled the warmth of the summer sun.

Entering the museum, Jeanile walked over to the membership desk and produced her membership card. Ravenell grinned as he pulled his own membership card and extended it to the attendant for inspection. Turning to grin mischievously down at Jeanile, he gently pushed her hanging jaw upwards in an effort to wipe the startled look of surprise from her face.

"Just remember - anything you can do, I can do better." And with that, he gently brushed his lips against hers and nonchalantly captured his first kiss from her waiting lips.

Even after she had recovered from the tingling sensation fluttering on her lips, Ravenell hadn't released her shoulders. They stood staring at each other, Jeanile trying to hide her breathlessness.

"Why don't you lead the way?" she finally asked, waving her arm toward the displays. It was easier to retreat than to stand there in the middle of the Met gapping at this puzzle of a man.

Ravenell gently took her hand and led her expertly through the maze of exhibits, pointing to the displays that he had come to recognize as his favorites. Jeanile enjoyed the fact that there was more to him than just playing football. Most of the pieces he pointed out showed more than just a passing knowledge of art, and she began to feel embarrassed at how she had underestimated him.

They journeyed hand in hand up the grand staircase to the hall of Greco-Roman statutes, through the darkened cathedral lightening of the Middle-Ages with its religion-influenced works of art. The light banter of competitive ideas about the works of art and the race to show the other that they knew something of the different masters colored their conversation for most of the afternoon. It wasn't until they were walking through the French rooms with its Louis XVI styled décor that Jeanile became silent.

The last time she had viewed these rooms had been in the company of Gary. They had spent the afternoon making conjectures of all the witty banter and risqué flirtation that must have occurred in the presence of the pieces during the rein of that most unfortunate French king. Gary had even managed to entice her out of her shell enough to indulge in some very naughty PDA with him. In all of her subsequent visits, she had purposely gone out of her way to avoid this wing. Yet now in Ravenell's presence the memory hadn't pained her as it normally did. The memories of Gary hadn't disturbed her yet, and they had gone through most of the exhibit before Gary had even crossed her mind.

"You're kind of quiet," Ravenell said as they strolled through the French wing, walking into the hall of the museum dedicated to the Impressionist period. The light pastel colored canvases blurred, converged and winked at the passing lovers. "Is something on your mind?"

Glancing up, she found him gazing intently at her. "It's nothing," she told him, instantly. "I guess… sometimes I just get lost in the beauty of all this." Waving a hand, she indicted that she meant the impressionist paints lining the walls of the gallery. She didn't feel guilty because of the small lie. It was the truth. The atmosphere of the museum, the people milling around with quiet reverence as they moved from painting to glorious painting, and the beautiful and priceless works of art had a different effect on Jeanile today than it normally did. It was wonderful to share art for art's sake, rather than sharing art as a means of foreplay.

He returned her smile with a slow, sensual one of his own, making her knees weak when she saw a dimple briefly appear. "I know exactly what you mean. After my mother died, my Dad and I went to live with his only sister, my Aunt Beulah. She nagged us about everything under the sun. The only moment of peace my Dad could find was out of her house, in the quiet atmosphere of celebrated master painters. We went to museums, galleries, libraries, ballparks, beaches – you name it. Anywhere, just as long as we were out of Beulah's house.

He was very good with his hands, too. It was amazing how he could fix anything. I was so proud of him..." His voice trailed off, as he reminisced about the times he would stroll down these same corridors with his all-time favorite hero. Jeanile was the first woman he had ever shared that memory with. He didn't like thinking about the misery his father had endured because he wanted to give his son a chance in the world, a world where the dice was already loaded against him.

His mother had passed away soon after his father had lost his job. Living with his Aunt Beulah gave him a chance to go to some of the best schools in the city. Beulah had made a name for herself in the legal world, but had sacrificed the chance to have a family in order to pursue her career. As a result, she gave Ravenell all the material advantages she could afford, but she extracted a heavy price from his father by never letting him forget that he had failed at finding a successful career. Beulah made them pay for their benefits by effectively killing any chance of enjoying a happy home.

"Hey."

The brief squeeze of Jeanile's hand was reassuring and comfortable, breaking him out of his reverie. "Why don't you show me your favorite spot?" she offered while trying to dispel the shadow that had passed over Ravenell's brow. She was touched that he had shared that memory with her.

"Only if you promise to show me yours," he replied.

"It's a deal."

She extended her hand to him for a handshake as a way of sealing the deal. With a sweet sense of exhilaration, Ravenell accepted and Jeanile couldn't help but marvel at his long, strong fingers and the fact that he didn't immediately release her hand.

"Follow me."

He hurried her back through the medieval art section with its dimly lit halls to the brightly lit American Wing. They strolled past dainty dining rooms, chairs, clocks and everything Americana from paintings of the founding fathers to colored and stained glass windows from the turn of the past century. Soon they arrived at a courtyard that was filled with statues by American artists. Ravenell pointed ahead of them a few feet.

"Okay. What does this piece say to you?" he asked as they strolled through the statute garden.

Looking up, Jeanile gazed at the bronze-colored statue of a woman's body that appeared to be stretched and frozen in a moment of ecstasy. She took a slow walk around the work of art to get the full effect. Gazing at the well-worked muscles from shoulder to arms as the graceful fingers of the statue grasped a bunch of grapes, her eyes slowly traveled down her long graceful neck, past her pert young breasts, her flat stomach, and long strong legs until finally she met Ravenell's eyes with a tinge of desire.

"It reminds me of being awakened and aware." Jeanile replied simply but breathlessly.

"Well, that's not exactly how I stretch in the mornings when I wake up, and I would be shocked if you woke up to the morning's sky clad." Ravenell teased as he folded Jeanile gently in his arms.

"Sky clad?" Jeanile asked.

"Birthday suit," he whispered quietly into her ear, nuzzling his nose behind it just slightly. He would not deny that he constantly thought of kissing her like this and letting the heat of the moment take over.

Giggling at the picture he conjured in her mind, she said, "I didn't mean *literally*. I meant it as an awakening because she becomes aware of the power of her body and she's aware that if she were fat, short, or even all arms and legs she would still be just as beautiful and powerful."

"So... beauty equals power?" Ravenell gazed into her soft warm eyes.

"No, the power comes from a belief in herself. Her pose says 'Look at me, it's glorious to be me. I'm young, agile, sexy and free.'"

"Well, that was a beautiful answer." Ravenell placed a gentle kiss on Jeanile's neck and was not surprised at the beautiful sigh that escaped her lips. It didn't take much effort on his part to turn her around in his arms and claim her lips with a sweet and tender kiss. Her arms slowly traveled delightfully up his strong arms to rest gently around his neck as she tilted her head back and closed her eyes in anticipation of the sweet sensation of kissing him. This was not a kiss to be taken lightly, nor was it a kiss that was given in the heat of the moment. It was a kiss that simply said hello and thank you for being you. A Public Display of Affection it was not. It was a kiss of satisfaction, desire and respectful homage paid to a sexy Goddess.

The muted sounds of the museum faded gently into the background as Ravenell drew her closer to his body.

* * *

The noise of the taxi cabs, the rumble of the subway, the jostle of the people, the sinking sun winking at them from between the skyscrapers and that strange bittersweet summery smell of New York all served to augment their stroll through the city.

The warm summer air tickled Jeanile's skin as she walked hip to hip with Ravenell down 60th Street. They had been walking for hours after they had left the museum, sharing memories of their childhood, family, college and work as they peeked through store windows and stepped into quaint out-of-the way stores with no particular aim to purchase anything but in the spirit of exploration. Ravenell would ask her questions about the things she showed an interest in, just to see her big brown eyes light up and catch the dimples winking in her cheeks. His eyes were constantly drawn towards her full lips, and every now and then he would give into the urge to capture them in a brief but exciting kiss.

"What were you like at nine?" Ravenell asked to distract his wayward thoughts. He had to get his hormones under control. If he didn't, it was very likely that he would scare her off by being too passionate before he had a chance to get to know her — and that was something that he definitely desired.

"Now I *know* you're a pervert," Jeanile giggled.

The question took her unaware, and she wasn't sure exactly how to answer it. She could blab about her childhood all day long because she considered herself one of the lucky ones. She had a good home, fabulous parents and supportive siblings. Even the teasing she had endured when she first came to America, with her thick Jamaican accent and behind-the-fashion style of dress, was something she could laugh at now. For her, it was a bit unusual for her date to want to know what she was like outside of the lust factor.

"I am a pervert," he conceded, "But not in the context of running around in a raincoat flashing people. I can imagine you in pigtails and showing your dolls how to invent things, or maybe you were already into mystery novels like Nancy Drew. In reality, you were probably a mean little brat who always wanted her own way." Ravenell smiled. "I just want to hear you tell me about you. In your own words."

"I suppose resistance is futile?" Jeanile asked.

"See, that's what I mean. You were a Trekkie. It's juicy bits of information like that that I want. It paints a rather delightful picture of you. A more complete picture."

"Not so delightful," she grinned. "I wasn't the girly type, playing with dolls and running around in pink. I was a tomboy at heart. It used to drive my mother crazy because I would burn the chicken, forget to add the coconut milk to the rice and peas, the whole bit. All because I wanted to be outside playing and getting dirty with the boys."

"Really dirty?" he teased.

"Really dirty. Mud, dirt, cuts, scrapes and the occasional frog."

"I bet you're a great cook now."

"You'd lose that bet. In fact, everyone who knew me would think that you're a sucker for even taking it. Instead of just burning the chicken, I now can burn the rice to perfection. And at the ripe old age of nine I was stealing my mother's romance novels and devouring them."

"I don't believe that." Ravenell said with a chuckle.

"Believe it. I used to sneak them out of her special cabinet and when everyone had gone to bed I would read the book with my head close to the nightlight."

"Did she ever catch you?"

"Yeah, but that was my own fault. One night I finished a particularly racy novel that was so good I didn't want it to end. I might have even thought that it was real. I don't quite remember all the details. All I can tell you is that my mom came into my room because I was crying and I was really upset, and when she found out *why* she *really* tanned my hide. Anyway, I went to sleep with few cares after that. Those books were off limits once again — I never found her new hiding place. My mom had straightened me out, but good."

"Do you know that your accent just spiked off the charts when you were telling me that story?" Ravenell commented.

Jeanile smiled. "It happens. You know the saying... 'you can take the girl from Jamaica, but you can't take the Jamaican out of the girl.'"

"Mi noh weh yu mean, mon!" Ravenell intoned in his imitation of a Rastafarian voice.

"You, too?" Jeanile asked, her smile so deep that two dimples popped out of her cheeks.

"Well, no, but I have a couple of Jamaican friends, and you kind of learn to pick up a little bit here and there," he said as he stared down at her.

"I should have known!" Jeanile exclaimed with mock disappointment. "Jamaican by osmosis."

"You're one to talk. Until a few moments ago I had no idea you were Jamaican. You have a very proper way of speaking, almost as if you were brought up on the 'Queen's English.'" He stated a bit distractedly. He was looking around trying to figure out where the music in the distance was coming from. He was desperately hoping for another excuse to prolong this date.

"Chat 'bout." Jeanile stated in her deepest Jamaican accent she could conjure.

"I don't have any Jamaican in me, but I have some Latino blood three times removed on my best friend's side. And, if I'm hearing correctly, we can always take it to the dance floor to see if I'm faking it."

"What do you mean?" Jeanile asked, trying to hear what he was listening to. The music was faint yet distinctly meringue.

"Don't you hear that?" He asked.

She cocked her head to one side. "Oh. Sure. It sounds like meringue. That's what I love about New York City - you never know what you'll find here."

"My accent may be off when it comes to speaking like a Jamaican, but Spanish music I know like the back of my hand. And that," he said, pointing toward the music. "That's salsa."

"Yeah, yeah, sure, sure," Jeanile protested. She loved a good competition.

"Regardless of what you claim to know, I know that that's salsa. But again, we can always settle this by locating the music." He raised his eyebrows by way of a challenge as well as an invitation.

"Lead the way."

They meandered down the side streets and main roads following the music. Its sound fluctuated constantly, sometimes sounding closer and then, seconds later, almost disappearing completely. "Why don't we just ask someone for directions." The unstated *'why won't a man ever ask for directions?'* was evident in the tone of her voice.

Ravenell playfully rolled his eyes.

Jeanile laughed and stopped the first passersby to get the necessary information.

"Excuse me. Can you tell me where the music is coming from?" She asked a group of giggling girls walking toward them, talking, laughing and walking in time to the music.

"Oh, sure," a bubbly blonde answered, "That's *Swing Time In The City* at Lincoln Center." Some of the others pointed them in the right direction.

Jeanile thanked them while flashing a smile at Ravenell that clearly stated 'I told you so.'

"Yeah. It's a lot of fun. It's salsa night tonight, but last week they had jazz." One of the girls laughingly told them as they separated from the group.

"Thank *you*." Ravenell called over his shoulders. He started to whistle under his breath like a contented know-it-all. Obviously refraining from telling her 'I told *you* so.'

"Okay, okay, so you were right. I just hope you can dance salsa."

"All it takes is a little rhythm and a twirl — just like reggae," Ravenell said confidently.

"I don't remember anyone twirling *me* when I'm dancing reggae," Jeanile politely informed him.

"That's only because it's very hard to twirl your partner when the DJ has already suggested that every body should 'wine an' go dun'!' he finished in Jamaican. The entire time they were discussing their options, Ravenell had been slowly directing their footsteps towards the music that was getting louder and louder the closer they came to Lincoln Center. Soon the music could be heard from all sides and they were able to see as well as hear what the New Yorkers called *'Swing Time In The City'*.

From the looks of the crowd everyone — including the amateurs — was enjoying themselves. The music was loud but hypnotic, dancers were swinging and gyrating to the sounds of sweet salsa on the makeshift dance floor while the bar stations placed discreetly around the makeshift dance floor was heavily trafficked.

"This is great!" Jeanile could hardly repress her excitement as she bounced enthusiastically in time to the music. They had barely made it to the dance floor before her hips began to sway invitingly in time to the music the live band played. Her hands and feet followed the gentle instructions indicated by Ravenell's right hand at the base of her spine, his left hand twirling her every chance he could.

Every time after a spin, Ravenell's hand would return to the base of her spine to draw her that much closer to him, and Jeanile marveled at how swiftly their maneuvers became synchronized to the point where they were able to move as one. The laughing crowd, the music and the heady feeling every time he drew her into his arms excited Jeanile's body to the point where her breath came faster and faster. Her nipples strained hard against the soft fabric of her blouse, and the blood rushed to her cheeks when she glanced down only to realize they were advertising her inner emotions.

Ravenell's gaze followed hers, but swiftly found something else to engage his attention. Although the reaction of her body enticed and pleased him greatly, he was too much of a gentleman to be caught peeping.

Jeanile knew she was attracted to him, but this easy response to his proximity was disconcerting nonetheless. Her eyes drifted slowly up Ravenell's body as she imagined what he would look like without his shirt. She was feeling hot and breathless by the time her eyes had met his knowing look.

She missed a step and he pulled her closer to break her fall. She was now firmly pressed up against his body, and intimate pictures formed by the feel of every muscle in his body only caused her heart rate to accelerate even faster. The feel of her soft breasts against his solid chest and the faint yet enticing scent of his cologne only made matters worse.

They had stopped moving, locked within the awareness of their desire for each other, completely ignoring the rest of the dancers or the speed of the music.

As if on cue, the lead singer stepped up to the microphone and the song came to an abrupt end. Everyone, except Jeanile and Ravenell, applauded enthusiastically.

"Okay," the MC said when the cheers had subsided. "This one goes out to all the lovers."

Ravenell opened his arms in an invitation and Jeanile moved the small distance into his embrace.

Ravenell released an unconscious breath when she gently laid her head on his chest. He could feel from the roots of his hair to the marrow of his bones that this was where he belonged.

The sound of her humming brought him back from his thoughts. It pleased him to hear her hum — a bit off key — as they swayed to the soft ballad. Without thinking, he found himself putting the words to the song.

"Y una noche al sin. La luna se encendio. Te vi fue magico," he murmured by her ear. "Hoy esta aqui. Y se que no te iras. Seras mi musica."

"Hmm. That sounds lovely. Does it sound as nice in English?" Jeanile asked softly.

"*And finally on this night, the moon is shining. To see you is magic. We are here and you belong here in my arms. You are my music.*" He translated in the same tone as before.

Jeanile stopped dancing and looked into his eyes. She was touched by what she saw there. Smiling softly, she simply stretched up, wrapped her arms around his neck and drew his lips down to hers. The fiery passion that came to life between their lips spread to their heated bodies with startling speed.

With a primitive groan, Ravenell drew Jeanile closer to his body — if that was even possible. The heat of her body, of her hands upon his frame stroked the passion that was building within him. His tongue licked her lips and traced their borders, begging entrance so that he could taste her sweet ambrosia.

A moan escaped her lips as she acquiesced to his gentle demand. She was so surprised by her body's enthusiastic response that reality came flooding back to her and she drew her lips away from his, severing their heated connection. The roar of the crowd's applause to the bands rendition of *Parte se mi Corazon* by *Sin Bandera* was like a bucket of cold water to her heated and over-sensitive body. She buried her head on his shoulder to hide her confusion and avoid his eyes — dreading whatever emotion she might see reflected in them.

Ravenell gave Jeanile's shoulder a reassuring squeeze when he realized that she was too embarrassed to meet his gaze. "I think we need a drink," he said tactfully as he steered her off the dance floor and toward the bar.

TRES

It had been a whirlwind romance and Ravenell wondered how they had gotten to be so close in so short a time. In the past couple of months they had spent every free moment together. Last night they had fallen asleep together - fully clothed – lying on the couch in front of his fireplace. Although the desire to consummate their relationship was a growing frustration that was almost to the point of driving him to distraction, he had decided early on that he was willing to wait. In many ways he was glad that their time together wasn't just about sex. He simply loved being with Jeanile and the void that she filled, that had been missing from his life for so long - a meaningful relationship.

Today they had decided to go horseback riding, and he couldn't have asked for a more romantic setting. The sky was clear and bright blue, the trees swayed with a gentle breeze and the beach was more than inviting as they rode side by side down the marked trail that led to it. The path had

narrowed a few paces back and they were forced to
slow the pace, with Jeanile taking the lead. His eyes
drifted hungrily to the sight of her jean-clad rump.
It filled out her pants to perfection, and the way she
straddled her horse brought some very tantalizing
images to his already distracted mind. He smiled and
shook his head.

Suddenly Jeanile's horse reared up, spooked
by a flock of seagulls bursting from the brush. In the
blink of an eye, she was face down in the sand, her
horse galloping a few paces ahead.

"Oh my God!" Ravenell said, jumping off his
horse. He ran over to help Jeanile up, fully expecting
to see a terrified look or even worse, one of agony.
He was pleasantly surprised when he saw her full lips
curved into a smile and her eyes dancing with
merriment.

"Well, that should teach me to keep my mind
on what I'm doing. I should have seen that coming!"
Jeanile exclaimed with a grin as he accepted his
hands, pulling herself up. Her mind had been
delightfully reminiscing about the morning, how
wonderful it had felt waking up safe and snug in
Ravenell's arms. His easy breathing had given her
the courage to explore his relaxed features. She had
been so caught up in reliving her visual exploration
of this morning that she had been caught off guard

by the birds, taking what she considered to be an amateur's fall.

"Are you alright?" he asked, bringing her thoughts back to the present.

His heart had stopped when he saw her fall. It could have been a serious accident, and the thought of her being injured, or worse - losing her - had paralyzed him for a fraction of a second. During that moment, the sinking feeling in his heart at the loss of her had turned his body into lead.

"I'm fine," she smiled. "I think that's a question you should be asking my horse." At the look on his face Jeanile couldn't keep her smile from breaking out into a laugh. She quickly busied herself with brushing the sand from her hair, face and shoulders. She desperately tried to brush the sand from her body but some places were hard to reach.

"I will, if I can catch him," he said. Unconsciously, he started to help Jeanile brush the sand from the back of her pants, but his hands stalled in mid-caress when he realized what he was doing. He flushed.

"I'm... sorry, I was getting a bit carried away." Ravenell apologized with a sheepish look.

"Actually, I was kind of enjoying it," Jeanile commented with a smirk. "It's not every day that a woman actually finds a knight in shinning armor who's sexy *and* polite." She delighted in the fact that she could pull the rug from beneath his feet with such a statement. And she was being honest. She really was enjoying his hands stroking the sand from her pants. *Lord, if only I could fall off a horse every day.* Jeanile smiled at the idiotic thought, the grin lighting up her face and making her eyes dance with delight.

Ravenell was mesmerized. He could feel the desire to taste her sensual lips building within him again. Unable to resist the magnetic attraction, he slowly lowered his lips to hers. The shock of delight tingled inside him as he placed a tender butterfly kiss on her waiting lips. It wasn't long before her soft body snuggled closer to his, enjoying the heat of his body and inviting him to delve deeper to taste hidden delights. On the sigh that escaped her lips, his strong arms drew her tenderly closer and the world spun crazily before it came to a halt, standing perfectly still. Her lips molded themselves to his and their hands, bodies and tongues began a tentative dance of exploration. Ravenell felt his body harden in response to the play of her tongue against the roof of his mouth. Desire, like warm, molten honey filled his veins, and he could feel himself tighten in response. He desperately wanted more of her.

Ravenell sighed deeply, shifting his body in order to gain and give greater access to their mutual exploration. His mind was racing with desire-inducing images: they were back in his bedroom; Jeanile was on top of him; her blouse had come open revealing her breasts to his hungry gaze; her hands were exploring the smooth muscled contours of his body; and he could feel his erection, firm and insistent, straining against the restrictive barriers of his jeans.

The seagulls screamed in scandalous protest as they circled overhead.

"Hmmmm! I think our audience disapproves," Jeanile said softly as she lowered her head to nuzzle in the crook of his neck.

Chuckling, Ravenell nodded in agreement. "I... um... I should go get your horse," he said. He needed to put some space between them, to get his body back under control. The sight of her standing there, her hands on her hips, nonchalantly waiting for him to fetch her horse made him regret the fact that he only had a few more hours to spend with her that day. Tomorrow he was flying to Istanbul to photograph a story that his journalistic team was working on.

*   *   *

"Well, if it isn't the prodigal daughter," Ramika laughed as she hugged Jeanile.

"I don't think the reference is correct," Jeanile countered. "I haven't squandered all of *my* money." She looked pointedly at the shopping bags at Ramika's feet.

"True, but I haven't seen you in a while. An' I *know* it hasn't been your studies that kept you busy, because Dominique told me that you've been hanging out with that guy we dared you to pick up at Club Envy."

Jeanile looked away guiltily. She hated the kind of women who dropped their friends when they had a man in their lives. Although she wasn't exactly in that category, a twinge of guilt crossed her face at the thought that she had neglected her friends.

"Wow! He must really be something!"

Ramika left her bags by the door and pranced over to the sofa, dragging Jeanile along behind her. "Well?" she asked impatiently as Jeanile looked around innocently, feigning ignorance.

"Well, what?" Jeanile shrugged her shoulders, fighting back a smile.

"Oh, *really?*" The skeptical look on her face expressed exactly what was running through Ramika's mind. Sex.

Jeanile felt the heat of her blood rushing to her cheeks. "We're just *dating* right now, Ramika." She couldn't help the guilty feeling that was coursing through her veins.

"*Dating,*" Ramika said, nodding her head slowly. The word fell from her lips with a thud. "And here I thought you said you weren't going to date any more for a while? What about all the high an' mighty, moral high ground stuff about wanting to '*find yourself*' before you jump into anything? Hmmm?" Ramika couldn't hide the jealous note that crept into her voice. After all, what did Jeanile have that she *didn't?* She had seen Ravenell first at the bar and had approached him. True, he had gently and politely turned her down, but as much as she liked Jeanile, she hated to think that she had been beaten at her own game.

Jeanile nodded. "That's true. I even stated that to him in the beginning, but he presented some very fine reasons to get to know him."

"Mm-hmm. I'm sure he did." Ramika stated as she fidgeted with a throw pillow. She narrowed her eyes and asked, "So, how was it?"

"How was *what?*" Jeanile asked.

"Come on, girl! *How. Was. It?*" Ramika practically shrieked. She was basically squeezing the life from the pillow that she held between her well-manicured hands.

"We haven't done it yet," Jeanile whispered calmly, trying to offset Ramika's excitement.

"What?!?"

"Well, how *could* we?" At the slightly incredulous arch of Ramika's left eyebrow, Jeanile decided to try again. "We started to date two weeks after the party at Envy, and then he had to go to Istanbul and *then* we had dinner with some of his friends, so…" Her voice trailed off at the tragic look on Ramika's face.

Without saying another word, Ramika picked up her cell phone and dialed Tracya's number.

Jeanile watched in sullen horror as Ramika invited first Tracya and then Dominique to come to Jeanile's apartment to hear one of the worst stories of letting a good man go to waste. It was then that Jeanile realized that not every friend had her best interests at heart.

*　　*　　*

"Don't you know the rule?"

Will skimmed the negatives of Ravenell's last photo assignment. He looked up when there was no immediate response.

"Of *course* I know the rule. Pass the three-month mark with no action and you're in the friendship zone. Man, *everyone* knows that rule."

"So," Will said returning his interest to the photos. "What's it like being such a good friend?"

"Aw, shut up, man," Ravenell smiled, shaking his head. "Seriously, the only thing I'm sure about is that there is *more* than chemistry! I knew from the first moment that I saw her, she was the one." He paced the length of the studio agitatedly. He wasn't the type to discuss his love life, but what could he do? He was in a precarious position and he needed some friendly advice. He was really beginning to care about Jeanile, yet every time they got really close — physically — she would always find away to distance herself. He knew it wasn't their chemistry and he knew it wasn't his body odor, so he needed some input from a friend to solve this very frustrating problem. He was on unfamiliar ground and sinking fast.

"No way!" Will said. "So Mr. GQ and Lord of Maxim is actually willing to admit that there can only be one?"

"Will, your clichés aren't impressing anyone," Ravenell growled.

"And here I thought it was bad enough that you wouldn't kiss and tell. Now I *know* it's serious. Let me guess, you woke up one morning and you were a new man? The world would stop revolving if you didn't see her or speak with her? Right?" He grinned devilishly.

Ravenell glared at his friend and agent of fifteen years, refusing to answer.

Will shrugged. "She *was* pretty hot," he said. Will had met Jeanile a few weeks ago when Ravenell had introduced her to everyone at Charles' birthday party. "But I can't believe that you're willing to go out like that. Rav, be serious. You're just going through a crisis of the chase. I mean, from what little you've told me, this is the first time in a long time that a woman's not falling all over herself for a piece of the Rav-master. The man with a woman in every port has actually been seeing... no, wait, *dating*... one woman for the past six months. You've tried all of your regular game—"

"Not game. I've never played up to her. It's genuine. I gave up my little black book to Steve—"

"You *what?*" Will almost dropped the photo loupe he was using to view the negatives.

"Well, I didn't think you'd want it," Ravenell said flatly.

"That's not the part that shocked me. It's the fact that you actually gave up the *Book!*"

"It was about time. I've outgrown all of that. I know what I'm feeling, and the Book would just be in the way." Ravenell sulked as he stalked back to the desk, absentmindedly fidgeting with a proof sheet.

"Hey, I hear you. I just had to make sure I had the facts correctly. You know how Sharon gets. She needs all the juicy details and she won't believe me when I tell her that Rav is a changed man who's willing to settle down."

"Whoa! I didn't say all of that! I just said that it was time to... to...." Ravenell was at a loss for the right words to explain.

"Yeah, I know," Will said with a gentle smile. "I was once there, remember? Now I have a beautiful wife and a baby on the way. Sharon still won't believe it. Do you remember how many times she tried to hook you up with one of her friends?"

Ravenell nodded, tuning his friend out. Will seemed to enjoy his predicament all too much and Ravenell wasn't feeling the sympathy he desired, nor finding the advice he needed.

"Don't you have to pick up Sharon?" Ravenell asked, glancing at his watch.

"Yeah. Listen man, I'll tell Sharon that you'll bring Jeanile over for Sunday dinner."

"I'll call you," Ravenell replied non-comittally.

Will grunted. "Yeah. Later, man."

CUATRO

"Congratulations," Ravenell whispered as he kissed her tenderly on the cheek. "Now you have a legitimate reason to get me on your couch."

"Just the couch?" Jeanile chided, playfully raising an eyebrow as she leaned into his strength. So often in the last few months she had been able to confide in him, and although he still chuckled every now and then about the fact that she wanted to specialize in sex therapy, unlike so many others, he actually took her seriously. She was thrilled that he was here to see her get her latest degree. And tonight she had every intention of rewarding him.

She smiled, thinking about her plans for the night and the painstaking care she had taken in choosing her lingerie. She had bought the lacy items the day before when Ramika had dragged her to Victoria's Secret to shop for "something a little naughty." Jeanile looked up at him and led him away from the party in the back yard to the after party on her parents' front porch.

"Trying to seduce me already?" He asked as he nuzzled the sensitive spot behind her ear.

"Am I succeeding?"

She laughed over her shoulder at his reaction when she leaned back into his embrace, and her soft bottom meeting the hard muscles of his body. His soft intake of breath told her everything she wanted - needed - to know.

"Yes, but what is the object of this experiment?" Ravenell asked as he looked around nonchalantly, making sure that none of her pesky neighbors were peeking through their blinds or watering their lawns.

"Remember when I told you that I couldn't possibly make love to you yet?"

"Yeah, after months of waiting, two overseas assignments, and many cold showers," Ravenell grumbled.

The tender laugh that escaped her lips caused his arm to tighten around her waist, drawing her closer to him.

"I told you how I had experimented with sex before, and that more than likely I would be considered a recycled virgin."

"Your way of phrasing things constantly amazes me." He snuggled closer to the nape of her neck for a few quick kisses.

"Well, you shouldn't be the only one with a monopoly on amazing people." Every time he had let her view the proofs from his photo assignments, she had been amazed by his ability to capture and convey a particular feeling to the viewer. He had a talent that was unmistakable.

Ravenell trailed stimulating kisses up and down the nape of her neck. His kisses were distracting her and the heat from his body was giving him a winning edge in their seduction foreplay.

"Of course, I went to college for my monopoly," Ravenell protested as he buried his nose further into her hair. He found the way the sun highlighted its raven blackness to be fascinating. Nuzzling and reveling in the scent of her hair warmed his skin and made his muscles tighten in all the right places. The strapless dress of molten gold that clung to the generous curves of her body made him tingle all over. He longed to fill his hands with the weight of her breasts. He wanted to carry her in his arms and lay her tenderly on his bed and see the longing in her eyes as he reached out for her.

"If you keep this up I won't be able to tell you my proposition." She looked pointedly to his palm that had been slowly making its way up her torso.

"Okay, then I'd better take a seat." He headed toward the lounge chair, but instead of releasing her, he positioned her gently on his lap and enfolded her in his arms.

"Well...."

The words she had practiced so many times last night now refused to glide past her lips, with her tongue joining the revolt by sticking to the roof of her mouth. Turning around in his lap, she placed her arms around his neck and leaned into his warm, inviting body.

"Jeanile..."

The soft way he pronounced her name forced her to moisten her lips preparing for the delightful feel of his lips on hers. Butterfly lashes fluttered as she closed her eyes in sweet anticipation of the molten heat that would course through her veins, making her body soft and pliable to his touch.

Ravenell captured her lips in a slow, sensual kiss that took her breath away. Jeanile could feel her breasts straining against the soft yet confining material of her dress, wanting to get closer to his beating heart. She wiggled her body to get a better position in his lap as the free falling of her stomach heightened the sensations that his lips were igniting as she opened her sweet nectar to him. His tongue delved deep within and coaxed a moan of pure pleasure from her sensual lips.

He thanked God that Jeanile's mother had a green thumb, successfully creating a jungle of ferns, daffodils, azaleas and rose bushes that now hid their very naughty exploration session from the prying eyes of her neighbors. His left hand caressed the smoothness of her legs as he slowly - ever so slowly - worked his way beneath the hem of her very short dress.

"Your skin is so soft." The tender note of wonder in his voice enticed a wanton purr from deep within her.

His breath caught in his throat when she placed a hand over his to urge him onward and upward. His right hand tried to keep them balanced, but when her nipple hardened as his hand slightly brushed against her breast, it became hard for him not to pick her up and carry her off to his apartment to have his wicked way with her.

"Jeanile?" a voice suddenly interrupted.

The distant sound of her mother calling from the backyard brought them abruptly to their senses. Ravenell gently but reluctantly removed his seductive hand from the hem of her skirt. They tried to straighten their appearances before her mother were to round the corner and get more than an eyeful of their passionate encounter on the veranda.

"Coming," Jeanile shouted back.

"Not yet," Ravenell chuckled as he took a deep breath to steady himself. He felt like a schoolboy stealing a kiss from his sweetheart while her father breathed down his neck with a shotgun.

"But tonight..." Jeanile promised, "We will have no interruptions." She reached for his hands to pull him up from the lounge chair.

"Tonight?" he asked in shock.

"Yes, tonight. I have something special planned for us, and if my calculations are right, it will probably take a while. I might even have to spend the rest of the night at your place."

Ravenell sobered up immediately. "Jeanile. Are... are you *sure*?"

She nodded softly. "It feels right, and I know it will be worth the wait."

Hand in hand, they walked back towards the party. Ravenell grabbed one of the Heinekens from the huge barrel on the back patio. He definitely needed something to cool his parched throat. Looking around the party, he thanked God that his thoughts weren't visible, because if Mr. Graham knew exactly what was running through his mind at this moment, he would probably chase him out of the yard with his cutlass. Ravenell had first-hand knowledge that Mr. Graham had a cutlass stored in his garage. Some time on his third visit to Jeanile's home, her father had called him out to the garage on some pretext or the other and had very casually - but deftly - used his cutlass to cut up some firewood. Ravenell had quickly gotten the message.

Smiling at the tight knit of the Graham family, he longed for his own again. But short of dying himself, heaven and his own family would have to wait. The Grahams were a great bunch of folks, and they had taken him straight into their hearts. Mr. Graham had warmed up to him soon enough because they had a lot in common - football, baseball and basketball. Ravenell didn't think that Mr. Graham had much of a choice, because he was stuck in a house filled with strong-willed, beautiful and opinionated women. The running joke was that he took one look at his youngest daughter and gave up trying to have a son.

Truth be known, Ravenell knew that Mr. Graham was proud of all of the women in his life. His wife had put her career as a public relations consultant on hold to raise their children, wanting to prevent them from becoming latchkey kids like her and her brother had been. Mrs. Graham never wanted that lonely lifestyle for her daughters, and had always made a point to be there for them when they returned home from school. Whether it was to put them to work in the kitchen, give them some playtime or make sure that their homework was complete, they were going to grow up with a hands-on mother in their lives. It was no wonder that they raised a computer engineer, a doctor-to-be and a shrink in the family, with only a few gray hairs to show for the many years of love and discipline that she and her husband had instilled in their home.

"Let's get out of here," Jeanile whispered in his ear an hour or so later.

"What will your family think?" Ravenell asked.

"Everyone will be nicely buzzed, if they aren't already, and with the noise level as it is, no one's going to miss us."

"But... Jeanile... this is *your* graduation party." Ravenell glanced nervously at Mr. Graham who was busy kicking some domino butt at the far end of the patio.

"That's a good enough reason to have an *after party* of our own, don't you think?" The mischievous light in her eyes was catching.

"Sure," he finally conceded.

He followed her meekly as she made the rounds saying goodnight to a few people.

* * *

Driving up to his apartment in lower Manhattan, with Jeanile sitting in the passenger seat looking adoringly at him had been paradise to him. They quietly laughed at the *clink* that came from her overnight bag every time he turned a corner.

"What do you have in that bag, woman?"

"Just a few surprises."

She smiled a secret smile and squeezed his hand with anticipation. She was amazed at the comfortable feeling she felt whenever her hand was enfolded in his.

"By the sounds of that infernal racket coming from the back seat, I would think I have some serious candle therapy coming my way."

"Nice guess, but it's not the candles that are making all the noise." She glanced nervously out of the passenger window.

"Lord, have mercy," Ravenell breathed. "Come on, now. What do you have up your sleeve?"

"Just a pair of handcuffs…"

"I know you're kidding." Ravenell gave her a furtive glance.

"Well, if men get to mark off notches on their headboards, why can't a girl master the use of handcuffs during foreplay." She teased.

"Jeanile! You are too original and wicked for words. I have to say, I would find it very hard to replace you."

"That's exactly what I'm counting on."

"Well, your job is done. Mission already accomplished."

"Rav, that was far too easy. And I haven't even mentioned the lemon and honey that I've got stashed in my bag."

"Lemon and honey… and what would you know about lemon and honey?"

"Well, Professor McGruder had a delightful way to counsel rifting lovers to explore each others body anew. Not that sex - even great sex - would resolve key issues in a problematic relationship. It's just a good place to start."

"You and your experiments." Ravenell shook his head and rolled his eyes in excitement.

"Hey, if I'm going to recommend it to my patients, don't you think I should give it a spin first?" Jeanile gave him a mock innocent look, as if butter could not possibly melt in her mouth.

"Sure. And lady, you can use me as a lab rat *any* day." He smiled at her as he pulled into the parking garage next to his apartment building. Giving her the keys to his apartment, he told her to go up while he took care of the car.

A few minutes later, Ravenell gingerly walked through the door only to find candles burning all over his very masculine apartment. The soft glow from the candles softened the straight edges and dark hues of his décor.

"Wow," he whispered softly.

He looked around the apartment until his eyes finally settled on Jeanile. Her hair was swept off her shoulders and revealed a very slender, sexy neck. The simple black nightgown that she wore accentuated all of her curves without revealing a shred of forbidden skin. She was all at once a temptress and a Madonna.

Offering a secret smile of anticipation, Jeanile lit the last two candles that gave his apartment a soft, inviting glow as she prepared to put her plans and props into action. This was one experiment where she was going to enjoy testing all the variables.

Becoming an expert in human sensuality definitely had its perks as she had carefully planned out tonight's adventure.

She turned to face him and realized that he had not moved from the spot since he had entered his apartment. His face was a closed book. Not a word had passed his lips since his initial statement of surprise.

"Rav?" Her voice was soft, uncertain, seeking his approval.

That was all he needed to break the spell as he closed the distance between them and drew her into his arms. Their lips found each other in confirmation of the heat that was building between them. The feel of the soft material beneath his palms drove his senses into overdrive. He had wanted this night for a very long time, but this was very much worth the wait as he lifted her up and laid her onto his oversized bed.

His large palms made their sacred journey down from her shoulders, slowly caressing the twin peaks that responded delightfully to his sweet kisses. His kisses blazed upon her heated skin through his lips as they made their way of worship down. Down across her flat stomach and to the crossroads that made her hips tremble with longing.

"As beautiful as this nightgown is - it's kind of… in the way," he grumbled as he fidgeted with the material while showering her body with kisses through the soft silky material.

"Yes," the sweet word barely escaped her lips as her senses danced with the passion that Ravenell was igniting. The liquid heat was building from deep within her and her lips were eager to feel his once more. Her hands trembled as they reached for him, trying to communicate her need to feel her skin against his. As he slowly made his way back up to drink from the warm ecstasy that her lips offered, he tenderly slipped the straps of her gown off her shoulders and helped her undo the buttons of his shirt.

Jeanile slid her arms around his waist and joined him on the tide of passion that the contrast of their bodies was creating. Her sexual props of lemon and honey were forgotten until Ravenell's hand knocked them over as he fumbled blindly around the night stand in search of the discreet, round wrappers she had conveniently placed there. Frustrated at the lack of results, Ravenell stood up to get a better look and in the process became further aroused by the picture Jeanile made lying on his bed, tussled in his sheet with the gown bunched around her waist, forgotten in the urgency of their desire.

Before she could notice his absence, Ravenell had located the package and was back in her heated embrace, capturing her willing lips in a passion-drenched kiss. She wrapped her legs around him in eager welcome and explored his broad shoulders with keen fingers. Her body was arched expectantly against his as her need to be filled by him exploded within her, filling her with an excitement that was almost unbearable.

"Honey," he admonished to her as her moving hips increased his overpowering hunger for her.

Ignoring his plea, Jeanile licked the nape of his neck in a demand of her own.

A groan escaped his lips as he felt the softness of her skin against his own, without barriers, a soft sigh of contentment escaping her lips. Her body was heating up to the brink, and still they had not consummated their first union yet.

"You're good," Ravenell moaned in desperation. He had wanted this to last, but at the rate she was seducing him he wouldn't be able to hold out much longer.

"Yeah, but tonight I'm wild, and I want you... need you... now." Her hand snaked down to firmly grip his member in an urgent plea.

Ravenell cried out as his mind and body reveled in the blissful feeling of slowly entering her warm and willing body.

Jeanile decided that she had waited long enough, and with a smooth twist of her hips she let Ravenell know what she wanted. With every movement of their hips the sweetest sensations exploded within them, driving them to the edge of ecstasy...

CINCO

Jeanile tightly gripped the romance novel in her hands, rereading the same paragraph for the third time. On the spur of the moment she had decided to bring it along for the trip to help pass the time. Now, however, she wished she had brought a *Stephen King* novel instead. The blood and gore would have been more useful in keeping her mind off of the man sitting directly in front of her. She had promised her mother that she would sincerely try to relax and seek some leisurely pleasure in the sunny country of Spain before returning home next week to resume the endless task of solving her patients' problems once again.

How can I possibly concentrate on a romance novel when Ravenell is sitting only a seat away? Her words bumped around restlessly in her head, and she feared the constant thoughts of him would bring on another one of her migraines. *Why? Why did it have to happen like this? What was he doing here?* She shooed her thoughts away with a firm toss of the novel back into her purse. At this rate, she would probably not get far into the storyline, anyway. *Where is Crime and Punishment when you need it?*

With a glare at the back of his seat, Jeanile decided that she basically had no choice but to ignore him and try to regain her peace of mind. She couldn't do anything about his presence on the plane - she didn't have a monopoly on airlines, after all. He had as much of a right as she did to travel wherever he wished. Reaching into her purse, she retrieved her U2 iPod in the hopes of drowning out her thoughts of Ravenell with the soothing voice, melody and words of Jill Scott....

*   *   *

What was Jeanile doing here?

Ravenell fidgeted with the thought. It was a long time since he had laid eyes on her - four years, two months and five days, to be exact. But he had never forgotten her and she was still as beautiful as ever. He remembered the first time he had seen her full lips and chocolate eyes, how her laughter would hover in the air ...

"Would you please fasten your seat belt?" asked a very deep, masculine voice.

"*What?*"

The question didn't match the memory. Ravenell stared blankly ahead of him, oblivious to the smiling male flight attendant in the aisle.

"Sir, would you please fasten your seat belt? The Captain has turned on the seatbelt light. It's probably just turbulence, so there's nothing to worry about." The steward smiled indulgently at the man who seemed to be having trouble focusing on his words.

"Oh," Ravenell said. "Sure. No problem." He started to buckle his seatbelt, absently coming to reality to deal with the fact that the woman who shattered his heart was now seated one row behind him.

*   *   *

His voice is still as deep as ever, Jeanile thought as she gripped her iPod while the plane bounced up and down. It was the kind of voice that has melted her inhibitions so long ago, and now not even Maxwell's sweet voice through her earbuds could calm the thudding that was the beating of her heart. She hurriedly scrolled down the playlist trying to find something - *anything* - that would block her five senses from the very handsome man sitting in front of her. Her restlessness was evident in the distracted way she scrolled through the selection of artists. Giving up on finding a song, album, artist or playlist to sufficiently distract, she removed her earbuds and stored the iPod in the seatback pocket in front of her.

Looking out of her window, Jeanile thought of the warm summer days she had spent exploring the city, along with Ravenell's body and soul. The memory of how his voice had melted her every time he was near made her squirm in her seat even more. She had once trembled with a fierce passion that only he could ignite in her. It would always be the same... his smooth voice making her as much a part of him as his body could. Those days were heaven. But they had also become her tormenting hell for many nights after she had run out of the church in her wedding dress...

*   *   *

Her wedding day had dressed itself in the beautiful Spring colors that were so prevalent in the season. The birds were singing and the sun was brilliant without a cloud in the sky. Everyone was joyfully and expectantly awaiting the beautiful bride to arrive, to sail down the aisle without a care in the world. But the stark beauty of the outside picture didn't help to offset Jeanile's tormented image the night before. The sight of Ramika walking out of Ravenell's room at three in the morning.

Now she stood at the door to the Chapel, waiting as the ushers slowly unfurled the white carpet that was the signal for her to proceed down the aisle and into the arms of her future husband.

She looked uncertainly toward Ravenell as he waited anxiously for her to join him. The smile he wore on his face caused her heart to sink and her nails to dig painfully into her father's arm.

Mr. Graham gazed over at her. He had been worried about her ever since he had watched her go through the motions of taking her bridal pictures that very morning. She had a determined look on her face that spelled trouble, but the sad vulnerable eyes couldn't lie. She had looked at him in a way that made him want to reassure her that everything would be all right. He had thought it was just wedding jitters, and decided to let it pass.

He gently tapped her to indicate that the music had begun and that it was now or never. He released a relieved sigh when she started gracefully down the aisle.

How can I go through with it? It would be like lying to myself. He cheated on me! And with her! Jeanile's eyes narrowed as she looked at Ramika, looking oh-so-lovely in her bridesmaid's dress.

Her step faltered as she followed Ramika's gaze to where Ravenell and his best man, Steve, were standing.

She is positively glowing! "The heartless bitch!" Jeanile mumbled as her fingers clutched her bouquet angrily. *How could he just stand there, looking so innocent?* Her thoughts whirled as she looked at Ravenell standing at the altar, patiently waiting for her to make her way up the aisle.

Last night she stood heartbroken outside of his hotel room door, listening to the sounds of sex on the other side, her heart wrenching inside her. She had been tempted to break the door down and put an end to their relationship right then and there. The immense amount of pain, disappointment and embarrassment had been the only things that had restrained her fury. Instead, she had made a resolution to confront him and give him back his ring when everything was over. So she had waited and waited for what seemed like ages. Finally, just when she thought it couldn't get any worse, she saw Ramika sneak out of his room and down the hall, a contented smile on her lips.

Jeanile's resolution had been forgotten and she walked aimlessly down the stairs, through the lobby and out of the hotel. She hadn't bothered to go back to her room. What was the point? Ravenell was sleeping around behind her back, and with one of her friends. How much humiliation could one woman take? Well, she had had all night to plan her revenge. It would be a little on the dramatic side, sure, but she wasn't just going to sweep this indiscretion under the rug. She would walk joyfully up the altar and publicly denounce him and his accomplice in front of all their friends and family. There was just one problem. She wasn't feeling joyful about it. Not at all.

The hum in the chapel brought Jeanile back to reality and she realized she hadn't moved any further up the aisle. Her feet had stopped taking commands from her overwrought brain, and now simply refused to move. The congregation was looking at her with concern, and Jeanile stared blankly down the aisle at the shocked look of disbelief on Ravenell's face.

Is it possible that I still love this man? Enough to spare him the pain, the humiliation that he had neglected to spare me? The words popped into Jeanile's head unbidden. *Love? After all this?*

Yes.

Jeanile stared at him sadly. She knew that she would love him for the rest of her life - despite all of this. Despite what he had done. She couldn't marry him, but the bitter, hateful revenge she had so carefully planned had suddenly lost all of its luster.

"What's de matter?" Her father whispered to her, concerned by the stricken look that was now permanently lodged onto his daughter's face.

She couldn't answer. Words - hurtful and otherwise - were stuck in her throat. Tears were now beginning to stream freely down her cheeks, blurring her vision of the people around her. She glanced down at the floor, and realized that an instant after hearing her father's words, she had absentmindedly dropped her bouquet in front of her. Then, grabbing the hem of her dress and turning around, she made a mad dash back down the aisle, hearing her name echo in the now quiet chapel behind her.

"Jeanile!"

The congregation froze. The voice echoed among the hallways, resonating among the shocked murmurs with Ravenell's utter pain and confusion. He closed his eyes as he desperately tried to block out the realization that now hit him. Jeanile had abandoned him.

Instinctively, she knew it was Ravenell, but she neither stopped nor looked back long enough to find out.

* * *

Jeanile watched as the old man seated next to her pulled down the tray on to his lap and generously spread his belongings out, either ignorant or simply uncaring that he was encroaching on her space. Normally she would have been fascinated by such anti-social behavioral patterns, but today everything and anything seemed to be getting on her nerves.

She used to love the take off of the airplane. The encompassing sense of weightlessness was usually the highlight of any flight, however, this time she had spent those moments reliving the bittersweet memories that has haunted her for the last four years. During the brief moment of turbulence she had strained to try to hear what Ravenell had said to the steward. Now she needed something, *anything,* to distract her from his presence. Even when memories of the last time she had set eyes on him invaded her peace of mind, it was apparent that Ravenell still held the power to entice her physically.

"Yes?" the man asked with a pointed stare.

"What?" Jeanile asked with a puzzled look.

"Young Lady," he said, "in my day—and that was a long time ago, mind you—it was not polite to stare." He returned his gaze to his tray and continued to arrange his items, making himself at home.

"I'm sorry. I didn't mean to be rude," she whispered, an embarrassed heat creeping up her cheeks. It wasn't the first time her cocoa-colored skin had kept "the woman in total control image" from crumbling.

"You don't seem to be the type to be rude, but I noticed that you seem to be a little out of it, if you don't mind my saying. You've been fidgeting with that thing every since you sat down." He nodded pointedly at the iPod she had hurriedly stuffed into the pocket of the seat in front of her. "Technology is supposed to make your life easier, but when you have too many choices it's *never* easy," he chuckled to himself.

"I know what you mean. And... I guess I *am* a little nervous."

"First trip on a plane?" he asked curiously.

"Actually, no."

"Do you fly for a living?"

"No."

Jeanile had already learned from experience that it didn't pay to disclose what she did for a living. On more than one occasion she was forced to listen to someone whine or even worse, describe in intimate detail the status of their love lives. It had taken everything in her power not to tell many of them *Welcome to the club!* Her own sex life had gone from bad to worse. Her heart was no longer in it because she had left that firmly in the palm of Ravenell's hands.

It had taken her a while, but she had come to terms with the fact that she would always have deep feelings for him. But that was the past, and all she had to do was to get through this flight, land happily in Spain to give her lecture, enjoy the city and catch her flight back home. Eight days. Eight long days from today. She sighed. The thought that Ravenell would also be in Spain at the same time sent shivers—and not all unpleasant ones—down her spine.

"Well, I used to be a plumber," the man said nonchalantly. He had taken her silence as a reason to gab to her. "Yep, I was a plumber before I retired. I'm seventy-two now, but you wouldn't know it to look at me, would ya?" He winked at her. "My wife was three years younger and she used to nag me constantly that I never take her anywhere. 'Ira,' she would say... By the way, my name's Ira." He stretched out his hand to shake hers politely. She took it, hiding her reluctance with a smile.

"Jeanile," she said.

"Charmed," he beamed. "Anyhow, 'Ira,' she would say in her whinny voice, just like that." He proceeded to imitate his wife's voice, which Jeanile had to admit *was* pretty whinny. "'You never take me anywhere.' I would have to tell her, 'Woman! I work all day to pay the bills, keep the kids clothed, fed, educated and the house together! I barely have time to take a...'"

"I get the picture," Jeanile interrupted him before he could finish.

"Exactly. Well, anyway, I retire and I figure now we can have more time together, because I loved my Bess. Her name was Elizabeth, by the way. A more beautiful woman you had never seen in your life! An' that's the truth! Anyway, so I go and retire, and not two months later my Bess decides to take a nap and not wake up."

"I'm... I'm so sorry."

Jeanile's heart felt a twinge as she watched the man fidget with the items he had laid out on the tray. There was a beautiful coral colored hair comb - the old-fashioned kind that women used to wear to pull their hair to one side, a dainty little handkerchief, and a compact. She watched as he reverently handled everything.

"Yeah. So am I. I was going crazy at home. You know, everything reminded me about my Bess. The kids are all grown up now, an' they don't know me an' I don't know them anymore. Everyone is into their precious technologies, now. I have to text my son if I want to call him during working hours! And my daughters are even worse! My youngest daughter thinks I'm morbid because I visit my Bess everyday. I really didn't like the way Marian, my oldest daughter, was eyeing my house and hinting that I couldn't live there all by myself. She's always had it in for me, anyway, ever since I told her I didn't approve of her second husband." He paused to wrinkle up his nose. "Lazy SOB, that's what he is." He shook his head sadly. "Anyway, I decided to take a trip, *all by myself,* and tell my Bess all about it when I get back."

"Oh, that's so sweet," Jeanile said politely.

"You fly all the time, right?" Ira asked, suddenly changing the subject.

"A few times a year."

"Are all the seats really this cramped?" He asked the question in a stage whisper.

"Generally, yes. Unless you decide to fly first class," Jeanile smiled.

"Hmphf. Well, I guess I didn't take my achy joints into consideration when I decided to go to Spain."

"It *is* rather a long flight."

"I just had to do it, though. You know, my Bess always wanted to come to Spain and see a bull fight. Her favorite movie star was Tyrone Power, and he did some movie with a bullfight in it and ever since then she was nagging me to take her to Spain. Then there was Casablanca, after which she wanted me to take her to Paris every other week."

"Casablanca is in Morocco," Jeanile reminded him gently.

"I know that, but she thought Casablanca would be too hot, so Paris was the next best thing. Anyway, these seats are just too cramped!"

"Well, you can always push your seat back a bit," Jeanile suggested. She showed him how to get the back of his seat to the reclining position.

"It's not my back that's the problem, honey, its my legs." he complained loudly.

Jeanile could see that the ride from hell was slowly becoming even more unbearable. Not only was she stuck behind Ravenell, with memories of him swimming around her mind, but now she was trapped with a cranky old man who was going to whine all through the flight unless he got his way. Jeanile breathed deeply, looking out the window as a means of escape. *This can't be happening,* she thought.

"Maybe I can help," Ravenell said over the top of his seat.

Jeanile looked up in shock. Her heart did a swan dive and her tongue was suddenly stuck to the roof of her mouth. She stared at him, speechless.

"Well, young man?" Ira asked in an irritated voice. "It's not polite to listen in on the conversation of others."

"I know," Ravenell apologized with an unrepentant grin. "I just thought you might want to know that my seat has a little more leg room up here."

"And why is that? Did you have to pay more for your seat or somethin'?" Ira screwed up his face and awaited an answer.

"Not at all. But I'd be glad to switch seats with you. That is, if you don't mind sitting close to the emergency exits. You'll always find more leg room around those aisles."

Ira's frown slowly softened on his face. He shrugged his shoulders. "Well, it's fine by me. That is, unless the lady objects. We were having a grand ol' time until my joints started to stiffen up."

Two pairs of brown eyes looked in her direction. Jeanile nodded her head slowly. She still couldn't get any words past her tongue and through her lips. In a very short time, Ira was sitting gleefully in the seat in front of her and Ravenell—for the first time in four years—was now seated mere inches away beside her.

Jeanile took a deep breath, steeling herself for an ordeal as she watched Ravenell smoothly folding his huge frame into the compact seat next to her. Unconsciously digging holes into the palms of her hands with her well-manicured nails, she waited impatiently to see what he would do next.

"Hello, Jeanile."

Hearing his deep voice intimately saying her name suddenly reminded her of those passionate moments when he would call her his *Wylde Honey*. She quickly closed her eyes to dispel those images - remembering was just too painful. Forcing her facial features into a mask of cool neutrality, she inclined her head in an impersonal greeting.

"So that's it? That's all I'm entitled to, after four years of waiting?" An angry muscle worked restlessly as his jaw clenched tightly, seething at her obvious indifference.

So that's it, Jeanile thought. *After all this time he would like an explanation. Well, tough luck buddy. That's one conversation we are _not_ going to have.* Her stomach churned with anger while her heated gaze gave him a cold once over.

He hadn't changed at all. His smooth, sensual smile still had the ability to charm. Yes, he had the most seductive lips of any man she had ever known. Full, bow shaped, sensual and strong—lips that parted naturally when he smiled revealing white, even teeth. Nothing about him was too large or too small. Not his eyes, his lips or his…

Jeanile turned her head swiftly to look out the window, silently hoping the clouds would distract her mind from mentally exploring his powerful proportions.

"I'm well, thank you for asking," Ravenell said, looking down at his lap. He persisted to ignore her silence.

The sarcasm that dripped from his hardened voice caused her to abruptly turn back to scrutinize his features. Jeanile felt her body stiffen at the hostility that shone from his eyes as he looked up at her. She knew him well enough to know that she had to change tactics if she wanted to have any peace for the rest of her flight. She took a deep breath and sighed.

"Hello," she said.

She couldn't bring herself to say his name. Her voice sounded unconcerned and disinterested, even though deep inside she felt anything but.

"Hello, *Ravenell*," he calmly ordered. His sharp eyes gazed intently at her features, trying to penetrate the mask of neutrality she had assumed.

Their eyes locked in a battle of wills as Ravenell waited patiently for her to comply.

"Hello... Ravenell," she said coldly. Her voice quivered, almost faltering on his name. For the past four years she had thought about him and imaged all kinds of scenarios of their meeting again, but she had never once let his name cross her lips. Her heartbeat now quickened and sunk to the pit of her stomach as it occurred to her that, despite everything that had happened, she might still love him.

"Thank you," he said with a self-satisfied smile.

"*Now* can we drop the charade?" Her tone echoed her bitterness, her typical smile now compressed into a thin, angry line. Jeanile's eyes turned cold as the anger of having her serenity disrupted by his presence seethed below the surface.

"As I remember it, *you* were the one who was always into games," he informed her.

She shrugged, willing to let that one slide if only to buy some peace and quiet. Deciding to escape this ordeal by stretching her legs, her fingers began to fumble with the release catch of her seat belt.

"Especially games that included running away," he continued. He grinned wickedly in his best imitation of a Cheshire cat when her hands ceased to tamper with her only means of escape.

"Okay. Fine," Jeanile snapped. "What do you want from me? What? Is it a pound of flesh that you're after?" She was secretly glad their reunion was on a packed airplane, because she was sorely tempted to slap the smug look off his irritatingly handsome face. As it was, she was more inclined to conduct herself appropriately in public.

"Me? Nah. I'm just trying to make small talk. To wile away the *five hours* we have left on this flight."

Jeanile's shoulders drooped at the thought of spending another five hours cooped up with him. It was official—she was now caught in the midst of her own waking nightmare. She felt her temples begin to throb as the onset of her migraine became full-blown.

In all of her pictures of meeting him again none of them had been like this. He was angry.

Really angry. But what did *he* have to be angry about? He had gotten off scot-free. The only humiliation he had suffered was to be left at the altar, and he had had the last four years to get over it. From what she had heard through the grapevine, he had even gotten married to Ramika, of all people. So what the *hell* did he have to be angry about? The words pounded inside Jeanile's throbbing brain. Her mouth felt as if it was filled with acid.

"How's Ramika?" Jeanile flung the words at him like an accusation while rubbing her temples with her fingertips.

"Ramika?"

He looked over at her, puzzled. Her tone and the question had momentarily stopped him in his tracks.

"Yes, Ramika," she repeated. Irritation slipped into her voice, unrestrained. She avoided his eyes, reaching into her purse for her bottle of migraine medication. The one blessing about the pills is that they inevitably made her sleepy. She desperately needed some relief, and would eagerly welcome oblivion if only to get through the rest of the flight.

"Last time I heard, Ramika was fine," he muttered.

"Last time?"

Jeanile absentmindedly popped the pills into her mouth and her eyes unwittingly drifted to his ring finger. She noted that he didn't bother to wear his wedding band. She frowned because two and two was not adding up to four.

"Yeah, there was some complication with the baby, but she's doing okay these days," He informed her nonchalantly.

"*Baby?*" It was more of a squeak than a question.

Ravenell looked at her in surprise. Gone was her cool mask of indifference, replaced instead with a look of utter dismay on her face.

"Excuse me. I think I'm going to be sick," Jeanile uttered as she all but stepped on him in her mad dash to get to the restroom and far, far away from him.

*   *   *

Okay, that didn't go as planned, Ravenell thought as he watched Jeanile hurry down the aisle of the airplane and disappear into the restroom. He had had offered his seat to the complaining old man in an effort to be next to her, hoping to start up a civil conversation. A conversation, he hoped, would eventually lead to an explanation. Before being seated, he had made a deal with himself that he was not going to beg her for an explanation. He was going to wait patiently until her conscience would naturally prod her to cough one up.

He had told himself constantly that when Jeanile had walked out on him four years ago, she was only running away from commitment. Not from him. That was why he had stayed away from her after she had returned his ring soon after the fiasco that was their wedding day. He had politely returned the ring back to her, silently hoping that she would take the hint and return to him. When that didn't happen as days turned to weeks and the weeks turned to months, he had eventually let the despair of his situation engulf him.

Ravenell frowned at the restroom door. *I didn't mean to upset her. Really I didn't,* he argued with himself. *It was unexpected. This whole situation is ridiculous!* His frown deepened as he continued to gaze at the door.

With a loud sigh he pressed his call button in frustration and waited impatiently for an attendant to arrive.

"Yes, sir?" The blonde stewardess prompted as she appeared in the aisle. "How may I help you?"

"Hi. Yes, I think the young lady who was sitting in this seat may need your assistance. She wasn't feeling very well and ran to the bathroom." He nodded toward the front of the plane.

"Oh." There was a look of instant concern on her face as she followed his gaze down the aisle.

"I don't think it's anything too serious," he continued, "but she didn't seem to be in good shape." He tried to shrug his shoulders in innocence, but they simply sagged under the guilt instead.

"Well," The young woman said, "Thank you for your help. I'll go see if there's anything I can do for her…"

"Thanks. And… before you go… could you possibly find me another seat?"

"I'm sorry?"

"Another seat? Perhaps in the back of the plane somewhere?"

"Oh, I'm so sorry, sir. We have a full flight today. I suppose I could check with another passenger, but…."

"No, that's okay. I don't mean to trouble you. It's just that I'd like to use the telephone, but I need a more… *private* line than this." Ravenell indicated the credit card activated phone in the seatback in front of him.

The stewardess nodded and looked past Ravenell down the aisle, motioning to the other steward walking toward them. "Well, I'm going to go see if I can help that woman, but I think Michael might be able to help you out," she said as the steward arrived. After she explained the situation to him, she politely excused herself and went to attend to Jeanile.

"If you would follow me, sir."

The steward motioned for Ravenell to follow him to the tail end of the plane where there was a phone situated in the wall. "This phone can be used in the same way as the one located at your seat. Just swipe the card and follow the instructions. I have to caution you, however, that if the captain turns on the seatbelt sign, you will have to return to your seat."

"I understand," Ravenell nodded, "and thank you." He waited for him to get a reasonable distance down the aisle before he turned and swiped his card. He drummed his fingers impatiently against the walk as he waited for someone to pick up on the other side.

"Donne Agency, how may I help you?" The very professional voice of Anna flowed smoothly over the telephone line.

"Hey, this is Rav. Let me speak to Will."

"One moment, please." There was a short pause and then the very agitated voice of his agent could be heard loud and clear.

"What's happened? You couldn't *possible* be there already, so what's wrong?"

"Nothing's wrong," Ravenell said defensively. "Well, not really. Look, I'm on the plane and everything's on schedule, I just think you should send Justin to cover this one."

"What?! Are you insane?!? Rav, you're not making any sense! I thought you *wanted* this job?!?" Will argued loudly.

"I did, but… I just… need some time, alright? Something's come up."

"What the—What could possibly come up halfway across the Atlantic in a plane?!?"

"Providence," Ravenell said calmly.

"Providence?"

"That's right."

Will sighed. "And what is that supposed to mean? 'Providence'?"

"Listen, Will. You know I've been working my butt off lately, flying here and flying there for God knows how long. I just need some time to take care of something, okay? If you can't get Justin or someone else to cover, then at least buy me a couple of days."

"This isn't like you, Ravenell. I mean, why would you…"

"I know," Ravenell interrupted, trying to avoid a long lecture, "but you're the only one who could make this happen, Will."

"Yeah, yeah," Will sighed. There was a long pause for a few seconds. "Well, I could probably get you a few days, but that's only because you're the best in the business. That, and they specifically asked for *you*."

"Thanks, man."

"Sure, I'll let you know by e-mail."

"I knew you could pull this off."

"Hey, it's not a done deal, yet!" Will complained.

"I know, but I have complete confidence in you. Oh, and have Anna cancel the hotel reservation in Madrid and book me one in Costa del Sol instead. And see if she can get me a list of conventions in the area."

"Conventions," Will grunted. "Any particular ones? Photography… Journalism…" His voice trailed with the distraction of someone taking notes.

"Yeah, anything to do with sex."

"Okay, a-n-y-thing to do w-i-t-h..." There was a pause. "I'm sorry, you must have broken up. It sounded like you said 'anything to do with sex.'"

"I did."

"Okay," he said, scribbling down the note. He paused again as he realized exactly what he had written. "Oh, *man*! Rav! You don't wanna go down that road again! That girl is *crazy*. Seriously, man. We all liked her at first, but look at the way she got under your skin. Walk away, man. Walk. Away. Jeanile totally wrecked you when she walked out. Don't you remember? Why would you even *want* to go there again!?!" Will preached agitatedly.

"Because once and for all I'm going to put an end to it. Providence put her on the plane with me and I have to see it through," Ravenell explained. "Everything happens for a reason."

"You're gonna regret this... "

"Listen, I've gotta go. Just do this for me, okay? I'll be in touch." Ravenell hung up the phone and stood there for a few seconds, staring at the wall, deep in thought.

* * *

Jeanile pressed the cold, wet napkin against her throbbing temples and wondered what horrid crime she had committed in her past life to deserve such torture. The thought of Ravenell fathering a child with someone else was enough to make her sick—really sick. She had made it to the bathroom just in time to suppress the uncontrollable urge to retch.

Gazing in the mirror at the desolate reflection of herself, Jeanile fought back the urge to breakdown and have a heartfelt cry. The ridiculous image looking back at her brought forth a fit of tears and laughter as she bemoaned her situation.

Some relationship therapist you *turned out to be*, she mocked at her disheveled reflection, her hands shaking as she attempted to straighten her appearance. *He is* not *going to get the better of me! I will walk out there and face him. If he wants an explanation, he will get one.* She hung her head in defeated resignation. Although her thoughts were brave, were strong and determined, her body and heart continued to rebel. A tear rolled down her cheek and fell silently onto the counter.

Damn.

Why Rav? Why? Why couldn't you have been faithful? Our lives would have been so different. Her dreary thoughts and invading memories of the past started to oppress her again. Sinking helplessly onto the only seat in the cramped bathroom, Jeanile hung her head and finally let go. She started to sob, freely, uncontrollably. The last time she had lost control like this was the day Dominique had told her that Ravenell was going to marry Ramika.

*   *   *

The bleak, rainy winter evening mirrored Jeanile's mood perfectly as she made her way up the steps leading out of the subway station. Huddling in her inadequate jacket to keep out the rain, she regretted not stopping long enough to grab an umbrella and a coat more suited to the soggy downpour she would have to endure as she walked the remaining blocks to Dominique's home.

She glared down at the battered envelope in her hand, the cause of her uncomfortable journey, gripping it even tighter in a futile effort to squeeze it out of existence. When she first received it, it had looked harmless enough... until she recognized the return address in the upper left hand corner. It was Ramika's. Upon closer examination of the envelope, it had soon become apparent that it was an invitation of some sort. She could also tell by the feel and the weight of the envelope that it was more than likely a wedding invitation.

She had immediately called Dominique to get the lowdown, but Dominique had refused to discuss it over the telephone with her. Instead, she had practically ordered Jeanile to show up at her place, ASAP. Jeanile agreed, but only on the one condition that Ramika would be nowhere in the vicinity. She had already fallen prey more than once to Dominique's inevitable need to have everyone get along.

Ramika had crossed paths with Jeanile only once since the shambles of her wedding ceremony. Jeanile's frosty manner had given Ramika more than a hint that their friendship was over, and not just "on the rocks," as Ramika had supposed. After that encounter, Ramika's unsolicited phone calls finally stopped and Jeanile thought that communication between them was all in the past. That was, until this envelope had arrived, staring back at her from her mailbox like a viper ready to strike.

Jeanile wearily pushed the ornate buzzer to Dominique's home and waited impatiently for a reprieve from the frigid weather. Dominique arrived at the door and quickly ushered her into the warm and inviting living room. "Jeanile!" she started, "What were you *thinking*, coming out here dressed like that! And in this weather! You would think that you'd have shown better sense than— "

Jeanile held up a hand. "I'm too tired to listen to a lecture right now," she snapped. "So just tell me what you have to tell me and I'll go back home and get out of your hair. Okay?" She reached up and started massaging her temples with a cold, stiff hand.

Dominique took one look at her bedraggled appearance and let her reproach die on her lips. Jeanile had lost a significant amount of weight since the wedding, and everyone who knew her could see that she was absolutely miserable. Dominique had watched as she had slowly cut off Ramika, Tracya and anyone else who had to do with their original group. She had even gotten a worried call from Jeanile's sister, Jessica, because her family had no idea how to console her. Their only solution was to wait with the hope that whatever had come between Jeanile and Ravenell would somehow be resolved, with everything going back to being the way it was before.

Unfortunately, Jeanile seemed to be most angry with Ramika. Dominique had been the only one to weather the storm and remain somewhat close to Jeanile.

"Well, at least take off your jacket and sit down." Dominique motioned her to the sofa.

"I'll stand."

Jeanile's hands tightened around the envelope, crushing it once again. "Dom, just say what you have to say and then I'll leave. Please, I have a lot to do before my sessions in the morning."

"I know. Work, work, work. That's been your constant excuse these past months, hasn't it? And the barrier you've built between yourself and the world is just getting higher and higher. Pretty soon you won't be able to get over it—even if you *wanted* to." Dominique looked at her friend with concerned eyes.

"Look... I know that you're doing this because you feel you have to, but..." Jeanile shrugged her shoulders and sighed, struggling to find an appropriate end to her sentence.

Dominique nodded toward the envelope. "I see you haven't even opened it yet," she said in a defeated tone. This was to be Ramika's last olive branch to Jeanile. It was because of her that she was getting married, and she wanted Jeanile to be there. Dominique had been charged with the duty of getting her to agree to attend. "Why do you hate her so much? What on *earth* did she ever do to you?" The question hung low and heavy between the two distant friends. "Jeanile... what *happened?*"

"Nothing I care to go into now," Jeanile said coldly. "Tell her I'm happy for her, but I won't come." Jeanile almost choked when she said the word "happy," and she had to turn away from Dominique's inquisitive gaze to hide the hurt.

"Ramika really wants you to attend. It's because of you that she met the love of her life and is finally willing to settle down."

"Don't you think I *know* that?!? Dammit! How can you be so *insensitive*?" Jeanile uttered with shocked, broken words.

"Insensitive?!? About what?!? Just because Ramika is marrying Ravene—?"

"Stop it! Just stop it!" Jeanile yelled, covering her hands with her ears. "I'm not interested! Just... just tell her and everyone else to leave me alone." She threw the soggy, wrinkled invitation to the floor and ran out of the room, back into the harsh, chilling rain.

*　　*　　*

Ravenell's lashes fluttered restlessly against his cheeks as he tried to fall asleep. The love of his life had fallen asleep and was now resting her head gently on his shoulders. The sight, touch and smell of her as she slept was driving his hormones into overdrive. Soon after his conversation with Will, he had loitered in the back of the airplane waiting patiently for her to return to her seat. Then he had casual sauntered to the rest room to give her enough time to settle down and compose herself. He had finally decided on his course of action, but for his plan to succeed he needed to first break down her barriers in the least offensive or antagonistic way possible.

His body filled with relief when he returned to his seat to find her fast, if somewhat fitfully, asleep. Slowly but surely her body had gravitated toward his, almost as if her unconscious mind knew exactly where she belonged even when she wouldn't have ever admitted it if she were wide awake.

He gently lifted the armrest that divided the two of them and settled her head comfortably onto his shoulder. His heartbeat quickened when she let out a restful sigh and nestled even closer to him. He placed a comforting kiss upon her forehead without thinking, and froze when she murmured his name.

Oh God, woman. Don't you know that you are a mighty fine slice of heaven? The thought was the only way to release his pent up emotions. He missed Jeanile intensely, and there was never a moment that she hadn't crossed his mind. He had quickly given up hope, however, when she hadn't responded to his note upon returning the engagement ring to her. She had casually left it at his office while he had been away on assignment, but he wasn't about to take it back. He had hoped his note of *'Forever yours'* would have said it all, but her lack of a response had quenched all hope of reconciliation. She had finally broken what she had left of his heart.

And now—after all this time—he was again holding her in his arms. He knew that he loved her, knew that she still cared for him—at least when she was asleep and her guard was down. He would have to use the few days allotted to him to convince her that she couldn't go on punishing the both of them for the mistakes of her past relationships.

He brushed a strand of hair from her face and sighed, mentally preparing himself for the Herculean task ahead.

SEITE

Jeanile stirred, irritably avoiding the sudden attack of daylight that streamed through the window of the airplane. Blinking rapidly to bring herself fully awake, she stared in amazement at the empty seat next to her and the human line of people slowly shuffling their way down the aisle and out of the airplane.

She had slept through everything.

Dinner had been served, the plane had landed and she had slept—quite soundly—through it all. She stretched and prepared to retrieve her luggage from the overhead compartment when the realization that something was missing hit her with cold clarity.

Ravenell was gone.

She wasn't prepared for the unsettling feeling of disappointment that began to brew heavily in the pit of her stomach. Turning her head, she casually glanced around the plane with the unconscious desire of catching a glimpse of him. He wasn't there. *He's gone,* she thought to herself. She bit her lip with regret as she took her suitcase from the overhead compartment, gathered the rest of her belongings and made her way toward the exit.

"Welcome to Espana. We hope you have a pleasant stay," the stewardess said with a smile as Jeanile stepped from the plane and into the gangway that led to the airport.

Jeanile flashed her an absent-minded smile that almost died on her lips when she suddenly recognized the stewardess. She was the one who had checked up on her when Jeanile had lost her cool in the restroom.

So it wasn't a dream after all, Jeanile thought, lowering her eyes in embarrassment. She managed to murmur a grateful "Thank you," as she walked away.

Only six more days left to go.

Somehow her desire to explore Spain and the excitement of the convention had died within her.

Her thoughts briefly flickered back to a time Rav had made plans with her to see the world together—back when their love had been pure, and theirs alone. They had planned to visit the Taj Mahal, the Louvre, the great Temples of Karnack and even the Alhambra.

What were his exact words? Jeanile thought to herself as she explored that delightful moment of planning the future, that night on top of the roof of his apartment....

It had been comfortably warm and fragrant that evening, and the stars had come out early to wink playfully at them as they cuddled together enjoying the pale, sliver of a moon, the warmth of their bodies touching gently. Rav had even snuck up a delicious bottle of Chardonnay to surprise her after dinner.

"I want to take you to every corner of the globe where they celebrate love. *That's* what I want to share with you," he had said to her as they toasted their glasses. "I mean, I might not be able to build you monuments, but I can at least take you to see a few for yourself." Ravenell gazed into her beautiful brown eyes and smiled.

"But the Temples at Karnack are not dedicated love," she teased, "and the Taj Mahal is a tomb."

"What better example of love than a peoples' love for their deity? The Temple of Amon-Ra is there, and that kind of sounds like the word 'amoré' don't you think?" He quickly popped a grape into her mouth to silence her protest. "Besides, the Taj Mahal is one of the greatest known and lasting monuments of love. A Raja built it in honor of a most beloved wife."

"That was so sweet." She rewarded him with a kiss and snuggled deeper into his warmth.

Ravenell waited for her to settle comfortably into his arms and then he planted a soft, tender kiss onto her forehead....

Jeanile stopped dead in her tracks at the vividness of the memory and almost toppled forward as a woman crashed into her from behind. There was a short grunt and suddenly the bundle of papers she was carrying dropped to the floor and spread out among the throngs of passing people. The busy airport buzzed like an active hive as present day reality slowly washed over Jeanile and she realized what had happened.

"I am so sorry. Here, let me help you," Jeanile apologized, kneeling to help the woman gather her things that had been scattered during the collision.

"Gracias," the woman said as she took the last of her things from Jeanile and hurriedly continued on her way.

Jeanile navigated the short distance out of the general flow of traffic and stood beside a row of seats, making a conscious effort to get her bearings and put her thoughts in some semblance of order. Her free hand drifted timidly to the spot on her forehead where Ravenell had been accustomed to kissing her, at least when they weren't in the heat of passion. It was a tender gesture that she had secretly adored, and one of the main things that had taken her a long time to get over when she left him.

Did I imagine it? she wondered. In her dream she had imagined that Ravenell kissed her there while she slept. It had felt so real, so natural and so very comforting.

"Oh, get a grip!" she chided herself out loud as she mentally pulled herself together, making her way back into the flow of pedestrian traffic. To divert herself, she began to make a mental list of things to do. *Get a cab, register at the hotel, get an itinerary for the conference, take a nap and then meet with convention officials....*

She walked out into the warm, inviting sunshine of Spain's sunny coast feeling confused, disappointed and alone.

* * *

It was a luxurious hotel, obviously made with lovers in mind, which would explain the annoying amount of public frolicking Jeanile had witnessed in the last three days. Everywhere she looked there were lovers holding hands, staring adoringly into each other's eyes and ignoring everyone else in the vicinity - *especially* the intruding, noisy convention on human sexuality. Other than the welcome dinner on her first night here, Jeanile had yet to actually dine out with anyone. It seemed her pensive, preoccupied mood had deterred even the more determined participants from spending significant amounts of time with her.

She had already attended three separate workshops, and it seemed the number of attendees was slowly dwindling. She wondered whether or not anyone would be left to hear her speech two days from now. Seriously, if only fifteen people out of a possible fifty-five had bothered to attend Dr. Garrett and his very moving lecture on erogenous zones and stimulants, then why would *anyone* want to hear her drone on about *anything?* Jeanile threw down her speech notes with disgust as she sauntered out to the balcony of her hotel room.

The full moon splashed its pale light on everything it touched. It illuminated the busy boardwalk that framed the beach, the medieval fountain that playfully splashed below her window and probably the lovers she could hear laughing just to the left of her down by the pool area.

Sighing, she mentally debated whether to eat alone again in the dining room or to order room service this time. She knew from experience that the rest of her party would be in the casino or in one of the many night clubs that lined the tiny streets leading down to the water.

Jeanile dragged her eyes away from the hypnotic moon when she heard a faint but firm knock on her door. Her features brightened at the thought of company, and she quickly pulled the belt of her robe tighter and lightly ran her fingers through her hair. Relief flooded through her as she scampered across the small distance to the door, joyfully calling out "Just a second," to the lucky conventioneer on the other side of the door. This time she would not say no, she mentally promised herself. She would do anything to get from within these four walls.

She opened the door. Her smile froze and her heart stopped.

"Hello, Jeanile," Ravenell said in a quiet, deep voice. "We have to talk."

The stern look on his face didn't detract from his devastatingly handsome features. Her eyes, the only parts of her frozen body she could move, slowly traveled the luscious length of his body, taking in every minute detail. She savored his clean cut features, the small sliver of flesh that peeked out from the collar of his cream colored button-down shirt that was neatly tucked into his khaki cargo pants.

Exhaling a pent up breath, she hastily gathered the neckline of her robe hoping that she had covered the engagement ring that she wore on the delicate chain around her neck. She glanced fearfully at him, hoping he hadn't noticed it, that he wouldn't recognize it as the very ring he had given her so many years ago.

Jeanile felt like a deer caught in headlights.

*   *   *

The flamenco dancers pirouetted, tapped and enthralled the audience that was seated shoulder to shoulder in the lounge area. When Ravenell had peeked in here an hour ago, it had seemed the perfect neutral territory to take Jeanile for a talk. He had been very surprised to see her in her robe. Her quick, reflexive attempt to hide the engagement ring she wore around her neck had only served to draw his attention to it. He recognized it immediately.

It was her ring. Her *engagement* ring.

It gave him reason to hope. No woman would wear the ring of an ex-lover if she were truly over him.

He had waited patiently for her to join him in the lounge, watching with dismay as the room slowly but surely began to fill up. Suddenly Jeanile appeared in the entrance, and he watched as she slowly crossed the room, making her way toward him in an exquisite dress of passionate red. The soft fabric ebbed and flowed with every sensual movement of her hips, and he was hard pressed to suppress the pleased smile that danced on his lips.

Now she sat silently next to him, pretending to be engrossed in the drama that was portrayed for the audiences' viewing pleasure. The guitar vibrated vigorously in time to the dancers' tapping heels and clapping hands as the female lead - caught in a love triangle - navigated her way between her rival lovers. The flash of her black dress and sweeping skirt gave the audience the idea of the agony of choosing between duty and passion. Soon the heat of the guitar cooled and faded, and she was suddenly alone on stage, to quietly dance a portrait of her despair and loneliness.

Reluctantly, Jeanile dragged her eyes from the stage. This part of the story was too familiar for her to sit comfortably and watch, especially with the man she knew she could never again have. She casually sipped her drink, hoping that he would start a conversation - *any* conversation. They had spoken civilly about their health, the weather and how lovely it was to be in Spain. Then the conversation had died a slow and painful death, leaving them in silence to watch the human melodrama played out on stage.

Ravenell glanced nervously at her. He could feel the heat of her proximity through his shirt, the smell of her perfume teased his nose as his desire for her gripped him tightly. He wanted her — there was no doubt about that.

"I'm sorry about this. It was much quieter in here when I first stopped in to book the table." Ravenell looked at her apologetically.

"Yeah. It threw me for a loop, too, the first night it happened. It's the custom here, though. They go to work, then have a four hour siesta, go back to work until about nine, have a lengthy dinner and then about eleven o'clock go out for a drink. It's a good life." Jeanile laughed.

"I love the sound of your laughter," Ravenell said, mentally kicking himself as the words slipped out of his mouth. He watched painfully as she tensed up, mentally preparing to shut herself down again. "I'm… I'm sorry. I'm not trying to pressure you or anything like that. I just feel as if there are a lot of things about us, about our past, that we have to resolve in order to move on." He glanced down at his hands, searching for the words, debating whether to reveal himself to her.

Finally he looked up at her, looked into her eyes. "Jeanile... I don't know about you, but I've never stopped loving you." He held up a hand to let her know that that was all he was going to say about his feelings for her, and that she didn't need to launch a lengthy protest.

Jeanile's eyes returned sullenly to the dancers on the stage. She watched as the male dancer favored by the female made his way back to the stage to console the lonely, desolate lover. She watched as the passion swelled with every strum of the guitar. She couldn't help holding her breath as he finally took her in his arms in an embrace that she found extremely sensual. Then she watched with dismay as the other male dancer took the stage, dancing in frenzied malevolence as he advanced upon the unsuspecting lovers. In a few heartbeats he would be upon them to separate them forever, either by marriage or by death.

"Please, let's go," Jeanile pleaded as she picked up her purse and gave Ravenell a look of desperation. She really didn't want to witness the severing of the ties between the two lovers. Not again. Not tonight.

"Okay."

Ravenell hurriedly dropped the necessary Euros onto the table, took her elbow and protectively lead her out the side entrance that led into the garden.

"Thank you. I'm sorry," she apologized, hoping she hadn't spoiled his fun.

"That's okay. But, can you tell me why were you so upset?" he asked, perplexed.

"I don't know... I guess I just needed some air. It's such a beautiful night, you know? It would be a shame to waste it." She walked with him through the garden toward the boardwalk. She was very aware that he still held her elbow protectively.

They walked in silence for a few moments until they could hear the murmur of the sea, saw the glimmer of the moon as it danced upon the quiet waves, the stark, salty air filling their noses with every breath.

"This is so very beautiful," she whispered.

"Yes, I know," Ravenell admitted. He wasn't looking at the sea, the moon or the boardwalk. Instead he was watching the way the corners of Jeanile's lips turned playfully upwards at the sight, the way her free hand went up to gently brush away the wisps of hair that were blowing in the wind.

"Jeanile...."

Her name hung tentatively on his lips. She turned and looked up to him. His face was inches away from hers and her breath caught at the sight. It felt *right*, being this close to him. Being here. Now. She closed her eyes, her lips parting in anticipation. She wanted to feel his lips on hers - *needed* the feel of him. So it was a shock when, upon realizing the kiss wasn't coming, she opened her eyes to find him a few feet away. She looked askance at him, a little disturbed at her own brazenness but also disappointed that he hadn't acted upon the invitation.

Ravenell interpreted her look correctly.

"Don't get me wrong. I *want* to, more than anything in this world, but... I think that... that we have too many things between us right now."

Jeanile nodded in terse agreement and started to walk away. *What a fool I am!* she berated to herself as she stalked down the boardwalk, looking for the beaten path that would take her back to the hotel.

"Jeanile, please. Wait. Just... give me twenty-four hours, will you? Twenty-four hours. Please. Is that too much to ask?" Ravenell had caught up to her and turned her around just in time to watch her blink back tears.

"No, what would be the use?" Jeanile asked as she stopped running, trying to hide her face and tears from his scrutiny.

"What harm could twenty-four hours do to you? We have nothing to lose but everything to gain. I promise you don't have to see me after that-if you don't want to. We don't even have to discuss anything that's too painful. I just... I want to be with you."

Jeanile's shoulders sagged under her own desire to give in. She wanted to be with him and Spain was too vast and romantic a place to visit alone. *Was twenty-four hours a lot to ask?* She silently argued with herself. *A lot could happen in twenty-four hours!* Her inner voice warned. *Yes but he did say that he hadn't stopped loving you. That was a huge admission for him to make.*

After much deliberation she turned around to find that he was so close that she had stepped into his waiting arms.

"Twenty-four hours," she whispered into his chest as she inhaled the earthy, clean smell of him as he held her close... close to his heart.

*   *   *

The guitar strummed whimsically as Jeanile, dressed in the same red dress, moved across the dance floor, her feet tapping out the beat of her heart to the plaintive wail of the vocalist. She danced as if searching for something lost—something that she had held dear. Her heart beat faster and the pace the guitarist strummed became frenzied in time with her desperation. Every movement of her body spelled out her yearning for Ravenell. She opened her arms wide to show the world how empty she had become, how much she need her Rav to complete his Wylde Honey. She stopped in agony when her need went unanswered. She searched the empty room. The vocalist wailed on.

Out of the dark, she knew his figure would appear. The guitar stopped and all three of them - the vocalist, the guitarist and Jeanile - waited with bated breath for him to appear.

Then she heard it.

The faint tap, tap, tap of his flamenco shoes coming in the distance, creating his own beat. Closer, closer and closer the sound of his dancing feet came, but always out of reach. Just when she was about to give up hope, he appeared. As fervent and breathless as she was.

The guitar started to strum. Gently at first, bringing them closer and closer to each other until they were almost touching. She reached out to touch him and he took her in his arms, his hands sliding down the length of her. Jeanile released a relieved sigh as Ravenell's lips finally claimed hers.

Wrapping her arms around him, she drew him closer until every inch of her was pressed against every firm inch of him. She whimpered with disappointment when his lips pulled away from hers but moaned with delight as they blazed a passionate path down the nape of her neck as his hands slid sensually down her back to settle on her firm behind.

"Oh, Rav." Her tongue licked his neck in response. She yearned for fulfillment. For satisfaction. She had missed this closeness, this yearning and release. Her hands explored everything within their reach, remembering familiar territory and aching to reacquaint themselves with his particularly sensitive spots.

Her breathing became shallow and uneven and her eyes became glued to his sensual lips begging him to return them to where they belonged - on her lips. Her tongue darted out to wet her own in preparation. The sight only fueled his passion to even greater heights. Jeanile stared, entranced, as his lips descended once again to hers.

The strumming of the guitar and the wail of the vocalist suddenly disappeared, as if blown away by the wind as Ravenell captured her waiting lips, parting to give him greater access for exploration. She could feel the heat of his skin against hers. He tilted her back and for a brief moment she panicked, knowing there was nothing behind her to break their fall. Her eyes fluttered closed as she gave into the moment and braced herself for impact.

Miraculously, they landed onto the fluffiest bed anyone could imagine. The kiss that had begun quite cautiously was now transforming into something deep, sensual and filled with yearning. Jeanile's greedy hands reached down to tug his shirt from the waist of his cargo pants when warning bells went off.

"I don't care," she whispered, trying to ignore the bells that were getting louder. "I want you... I've never stopped wanting you."

Ravenell stared at her as he started to fade away. The more she tried to hold onto him, the faster he was disappearing. She was terrified, desperate, but still she struggled to keep hold of him. The persistent ringing wasn't stopping, and it finally became so insistent that Jeanile had to open her eyes.

Ravenell was gone.

She was all alone again.

She sat up in bed bewildered and realized that the ringing was the screaming telephone on the nightstand next to her bed. "Oh God! It was all a dream." She reached over and gingerly picked up the handset.

"Hello?"

"Good morning, sleepy head. Times a wasting, and you promised me twenty-four hours."

"Um... Okay." She tried to suppress the yawn that slipped out.

"Well, don't sound so enthused," Ravenell complained with a delighted laugh.

"It's not that. It's just that it looks dark outside. When you said twenty-four hours, I didn't think you meant it *literally*."

"Well, it's five-thirty now, so we need to get a move on if we're going to make it there in time."

"Make it where in time?" Jeanile stretched, intrigued by the infectious gaiety in his tone.

"The Alhambra," he whispered.

Jeanile paused. She sat up abruptly. "The what?" she asked. The memory of the night he had promised to show her the world was not far from her mind.

"The Alhambra," he repeated.

Jeanile gulped. She was wide awake now. "But... that's in Grenada, and a good three hours away." She knew the distance because she had asked the concierge for information about tours going to the famous Moorish palace a few days ago.

"Well, then, I suggest you get out of bed or I'll be forced to come up there and get you out," he ordered playfully.

Jeanile laughed. "Aye aye, Captain. I'm on my way," she said, scampering out of bed. She replaced the receiver onto the cradle and smiled.

Twenty-four glorious hours, she thought.

She was determined make the most of them.

OCHO

The day had been spent pleasantly walking through rooms with beautifully decorated walls. The floors were well polished and the hushed and awed voices of the visitors to the Alhambra made it seem as if it were a place of worship instead of long unused palace. The tour guide was friendly and knowledgeable in the history of this magnificent Spanish palace that was the last Moorish stronghold during the reign of Queen Isabella and King Ferdinand.

Jeanile had long since given up on keeping track of the history of the palace in favor of admiring the ornate decoration of the walls and ceilings, marveling at the craftsmanship in a time when technology was so limited. Each room was even more magnificent than the last. The courtyards that connected them projected an aura of tranquility that had not been diminished over time, despite the various reversals of fortune that the palace had suffered. Nor did the millions of visitors that trampled through its confines every year subtract from the structure's formidable power. The ingenuity of the palace and its outlying gardens and buildings were nothing short of astounding.

Jeanile had lingered behind the others in order to admire the ceiling that the tour guide had described, in detail, as a replica of the starry sky as it was visible during the time of the Moors who occupied the palace centuries ago. She gazed in wonder at the beautiful ceiling, trying to imagine how much more beautiful it must have been when it was freshly painted.

"What does it remind you of?"

Ravenell had said it in a whisper, just above her right ear as he quietly approached her from behind. She was neither surprised nor threatened by his close proximity to her body, because throughout the entire tour he hadn't been more than a hair's breadth away from her.

"Our night on the top of your roof. When we planned..."

Her voice drifted away into nothingness when she realized just what her statement implied. It was one thing to constantly think about him and the precious days they had spent together in the past, it was quite another entirely to let him know. Now. In person. The knowledge of her slip mortified her, but she could not - would not - complete her sentence.

"Yes. Yes it does, doesn't it?"

He wasn't gazing at the ceiling, however, but at her beautiful, enticing profile instead. He was inches away from her, but with every breath she took he came closer and closer until their bodies touched. She could barely keep her head from succumbing to the growing desire to rest on his firm, broad shoulders.

Being this close to him again felt absolutely incredible, and the only reason she remembered to breathe was because of the simple, hypnotic movement of his chest against her back. There, in the quiet of the darkened, empty room with the stars shining gloriously above them, it felt as if they were the only two left in the universe. Everything disappeared for them except the electric currents of pleasure that tingled throughout their bodies, erupting every few seconds into white hot heat every time their bodies touched.

The shivers of excitement were followed by anticipation of the inevitable. In a moment of weakness, she gratefully rested her head on his shoulders and marveled at the frantic rate of her heartbeat, especially when his hand settled comfortably on the small of her back while gently turning her to face him. As strange as the moment was, she couldn't deny that it felt right. As if this was where they belonged — in the arms of each other.

Ravenell turned her tenderly to face him, and her eyes fluttered with expectation as she watched his lips descend, ever so slowly, to hers.

Jeanile surrendered willingly, standing on the tips of her toes in order to indulge in the taste of his lips that much faster. Her body merged into his with a soft sigh of desire, her hands roaming his body to explore the familiar territory with renewed eagerness. His scent was absolutely intoxicating, and the feel of his stubbled cheek on the palm of her hands made her legs weak. Ravenell caressingly pulled her closer to steady her balance, never breaking the delicious contact of her soft lips upon his.

"And here we enter the chamber of the Sister. Note the intricate detail involved in the.... oh, my...."

The voice of the tour guide trailed off at the sight of the couple lost in a passionate embrace. The woman cleared her throat loudly, her group of teenagers giggling at the astonished look of the couple that had been momentarily mirrored on the face of their guide. The man was the first to recover as he made their apologies and steered his partner in crime through the mass of giggling school children in search of their own tour group.

*   *   *

Laughing at the picture they must have made, Jeanile and Ravenell strolled into the Lion Courtyard to gaze at the beautifully arched column that surrounded the picturesque garden.

"Have you had enough?" Ravenell asked as he nonchalantly pulled her hand through the crook of his arm.

"Of this garden, or the Alhambra itself?" Jeanile asked.

Ravenell shrugged. Last night he had carefully planned what the twenty-four hours would have been like, but now his plan seemed stilted and contrived. He preferred to play out the rest of the day by ear. Just spending time in her company was enough for him and, with any luck, he might even convince her to spend the next day - and the day after that and all the rest of their days - together. Despite everything, he still wanted - still *needed* - to be a part of her life.

"As beautiful as this place is, I think I would like to sit down and rest," Jeanile commented.

"Well, let's see if we can find some lunch. There's a nice café in the plaza, not far from here."

"Rav...."

Her voice trailed off as she suddenly realized that she had used her nickname for him. She hadn't called him that in years, and she was a bit embarrassed at the thought that she probably had no right to call him that.

"Yes?" he asked. He completely ignored the uncomfortable look on her face, and smiled encouragingly at her instead.

"I... I think I would prefer something off the beaten path, to be honest. Milling around with the tourist from room to room and then sitting down to lunch with them... it's just not my idea of fun."

"I know what you mean. Did you see the lady with the shirt that said 'Jesus is my homeboy!'?"

Jeanile stifled a laugh. "It's called freedom of speech."

"Hey, I understand that, and I'm all for it. But would you in all decency wear that to what used to be the center of the Muslim world?" Ravenell teased.

"Well, you're forgetting the fact that it's no longer a Muslim stronghold. In fact, it was converted and sanctified as a Christian chapel during the reign of the Catholic Spanish Kings centuries ago. If Lord Byron can scribble graffiti on its walls, I think Susie Q from the Bible Belt, USA, can wear her 'Jesus is my homeboy' T-shirt, right?"

Ravenell laughed. "I suppose you're right..."

They meandered through the rest of the vast collection of buildings, gardens and stone arches that made up the stronghold of the Alhambra, finally making their way out to the street below. The sights and sounds of a thriving tourist attraction could be heard as they wandered through the tiny side streets that surrounded the Citadel. Rows upon rows of whitewashed houses lined the street and byways, the noise of neighbors calling across to each other and the smell of the market just ahead of them fueled the conversation for the rest of their walk down to the plaza.

Every now and then, Ravenell would point out something of interest to illicit her opinion. For the most part they debated whether or not they wanted to try a seafood café or something a bit more traditional.

"Nope," Jeanile said, vigorously shaking her head. "I was told that the pizza made anywhere other than New York sucks."

"Okay, so we won't be adventurous and try Romano's Pizza. Although I think Romano's is Spanish for Ray."

"Yeah, and every pizza shop has to belong to a Ray, right?"

"Okay. What the lady wants, the lady gets. Paella it is. Although I have to warn you that it isn't the same as the ones you'd get back in Spanish Harlem."

"And when did *you* get to be such an expert on Spanish cuisines?" Jeanile asked teasingly.

"Well when you're constantly flying from place to place, sleeping at different hotels and living out of your suitcase you come to develop a sixth sense about these things. I've basically spent the last year working around the world, and it is my concerted opinion that, because of the melting pot of cultures that exists in New York, the ethnic foods you find there are *always* better than the ones you find in the land of origin."

"Oh," Jeanile said quietly.

"You... seem surprised." Ravenell commented on her brief but non-committal response.

"Well... it's just... for someone who was as family oriented as you were when...." Jeanile bit her lip, for fear of finishing her sentence.

"When we were together?" Ravenell suggested innocently.

Jeanile nodded. She had lost her train of thought, and a small frown of concentration now marred her forehead.

"You were going to say that for someone who was really into family, why do I spend most of my time traveling around the world covering different stories?"

Jeanile nodded again, uncomfortably. She hadn't wanted to inquire as to how he had spent the past four years without her. Her imagination had done quite well for her by filling in the sordid details.

"Well, what's a man to do to keep busy, right? I needed to occupy my time to keep sane. My home life was driving me insane, and the only solace I found was behind the camera." His description of his present life was said without malice, and Jeanile found herself pitying him for the situation that he had embroiled himself in. Obviously he wasn't happy with Ramika, and preferred to spend as much time away from her as possible.

Jeanile gazed at a menu displayed in front of a small, somewhat deserted café. "This one looks good." She said it abruptly, as a way of changing the conversation. She didn't want to feel sorry for him. That would be the beginning of the end. She was having such a great time with him that she had to physically remind herself that this was not a date. He was married, and she was supposed to be miserable.

Unfortunately, the memory of the kiss they shared in the Alhambra, the easy way they had of talking together - as if the past four years had never taken place - and the beautiful, sun-drenched day was making it hard for Jeanile to keep her hormones from running away with her emotions. On several occasions she found that her gaze had settled unconsciously on his sensual lips, her mind wandering down the very dangerous path of desiring to have those same lips capture hers again, lovingly, passionately.

"If wishes were Euros...." she sighed beneath her breath as they took their seats and motioned the waiter for a menu.

* * *

"Jeanile?" Ravenell said quietly as he parked the car in the guest parking lot of her hotel.

"Mmm?"

She drowsily opened her eyes only to realize that the car had stopped completely and the sun was already well below the horizon, leaving only the faintest traces of pink and purple in the wake of its desertion. She sat up slowly, rubbing her eyes. "How long have I been out?" she asked, a bit dazed and confused.

"For most of the way back." Ravenell laughed at the look of dismay that crossed her features.

"Well, it's *your* fault for bringing the pillow in the first place," she accused jokingly as she tossed the soft but offending object onto the back seat of the car.

Ravenell shrugged in amusement. "And, like the last time, you were out before I could put the car into gear." He grinned wickedly.

"I'm sorry," she apologized sincerely. His smile was infectious, and she couldn't resist the urge to smile in return. Then she frowned. "What last time?"

"Remember the time we took a trip upstate to Bear Mountain?"

"Yes," Jeanile replied breathlessly as the memory of that perfect day washed over her. Her eyes sought his and her breath caught in her throat at the intensity of his burning gaze. She opened the passenger door and stepped quickly outside and into the refreshing air.

"You were so sore from sleeping the couple of hours it took us to make our way through the New York City traffic to the peaceful mountain road. You were out like a light before I could hit the accelerator."

"Hence, the pillow this time." Jeanile mumbled as she took his hand and strolled with her toward the hotel.

"That's right. I wanted to make sure that you were comfortable. I didn't want an ache in your neck to spoil the rest of the trip.... We have so few hours left," he whispered as he opened the lobby doors for her.

"I'm... sorry."

Jeanile swallowed hard. She had been thinking the very same thing, and now she had slept away a few of the precious hours she had to spend in his company. To break up the silence, she made an apologetic gesture with a wave of her hand that held a very rumpled map of the southern parts of Spain. "I wanted to help you navigate," she mumbled. It was the only thing she could think to say. The tone of his words suggested that there were a lot of things that his body wanted to do with her body. The thought sent shivers running up and down her spine.

"No, it was fine. I figured the last cathedral was a bit much, so you definitely needed your rest. Besides, I missed watching you sleep." He reached over and caressed her mused hair. In the few hours after their short lunch break they had become much closer. Jeanile had given into her desire to revel in his strong, sensual kisses and, as if by agreement, the past and the future had been banished altogether, giving them enough leeway to get reacquainted and to enjoy each other's company once again.

They entered the elevator arm in arm and Ravenell pushed the button for her floor. He turned to face her just in time to catch the look of aching desire she had directed his way when his back was turned.

Ravenell drew her across the small space that had separated them and into his arms. Without a moment's hesitation, Jeanile's mouth opened in ready anticipation as she drew his head down to give him better access to her lips. Everywhere their bodies touched created the excited feeling of instant fire. Jeanile felt the white heat of their desire course throughout her body as his hand slipped into her hair and gently caressed her.

A bell dinged loudly. She moaned, realizing they had reached her floor and that their lips would have to part.

Ignoring the bell, Ravenell lifted her into his arms and carried her off the elevator and through a small, shocked audience of onlookers. He lifted her as if she weighed less than a bag of feathers and only broke the connection of their lips to make sure that they were headed in the right direction to her room.

Fumbling with the key card, he swore with quiet frustration as he placed her gently on her feet. He finally opened the door and they stumbled inside, shutting it quickly as Ravenell encircled her with his strong arms again. Jeanile found herself pressed firmly up against the door, Ravenell's mouth and hands were everywhere at once. Jeanile's hands eagerly kept pace with his. The dim light that filtered through the windows was all the illumination they needed. In their desperate struggle to stick close to each other's body, they hadn't even moved beyond the doorway.

They tugged at each other's clothing, hoping to find some small release from the feel of bare skin upon skin. Ravenell trailed intoxicating kisses down the nape of her neck and he reveled as a moan of delight reluctantly crossed her lips.

"You are my Wylde Honey, aren't you?" he demanded seductively against her lips.

"Yes," she whispered as her lips sought his for satisfaction. She trembled as her fingers fumbled with the buttons of his shirt. Her skin burned with the desire that the touch of his lips was igniting within her.

"Please. I want you. Now." He growled apologetically as she wiggled provocatively out of her jeans.

"Yes," she sighed, covering his mouth with hers. She thought she would die of her longing to be possessed by him. She desperately needed and wanted him now. As if to indicate that need, Jeanile tipped her head back, ignoring the proximity of the hotel door and slid her hands into his hair drawing his face down to hers. Her lips danced playfully, ardently on his, teasing them softly and then provocatively opening to invite him to delve deeper. Ravenell was having none of that. Instead he drew her bottom lip into his mouth.

At her indelicate moan, Ravenell gave up all desire to tease and gathered her into his arms, covering her mouth with his. Jeanile opened to him like a blossoming flower, welcoming the kiss of the sun. Eagerly, wantonly, she slid her tongue forward to meet his, reveling in the delight of the passionate tango of their tongues.

Bracing herself by his shoulders, Jeanile reached up and wrapped her legs around his waist. An answering moan of yearning shuddered through Ravenell's body and echoed through her own. He caught her derrière, holding her firmly against him and then stumbled through the darkened room trying to locate her bed. Leaving her briefly, Ravenell shrugged quickly out of the rest of his clothing.

"Now," Jeanile begged, reaching out in the dark for the warmth of his body.

Ravenell groaned as he felt her warm palms splayed across his chest and slowly make their way down to the flat of his stomach.

"I knew you felt the same way," he gasped as the welcoming softness of her body loosened his tongue. "I knew that you couldn't deny our desire for each other," he said into her ear. "After all, you're still wearing our ring." His head bent down, trailing warm kisses around the ring nestled at her throat.

Jeanile felt herself stiffen at his words. The reason for the ring being around her neck instead of on her finger seeped into her bones, chilling her spirit, effectively strangling her need for him. Yes, she had doped herself into conveniently ignoring the fact that he had a wife to return to. Yet all this time he had been plotting to get her into this very position — vulnerable and on her back! The words pounded incessantly within her brain. *He's a cheater, and you're no better!*

"I can't do this," Jeanile said as she sprang off the bed with lightening speed, as if the fires of Hell were licking at her heels. With stiff fingers and shaking hands, Jeanile rapidly gathered her discarded clothes and began putting them on.

"What? What's wrong? I thought we were finally getting somewhere," Ravenell said as he sat on the bed in stunned disbelief, slowly adjusting his eyes to the darkness.

"That's all fine and good, but I wonder if your wife would think the same." The words were bitter and angry and the sharpness of them hung in the air between them like an iceberg, cold and ominous.

NUEVE

"My *WHAT?!?*"

Ravenell jumped off the bed, switched on the lights and stood before Jeanile as naked as the day God had blessed him.

Unable to meet his eyes - for her own were trained on all the gloriously exposed parts of his body—Jeanile was barely able to speak. "Your...your wife...Ramika," she stuttered.

"Wh-? *Ramika?!?* What in the *blazing hell* are you talking about, woman?" He placed his hands imposingly on his hips and glared at her from across the room.

"Ramika? As in, the woman you're married to and my one-time friend!?! Although she couldn't have been much of a friend since she..." Jeanile paused, trying to choke back the tears. "Since she did what she did..." Her words tripped over each other until they came to a halting stop. She didn't understand the look of confusion on his face. Why was it so hard to understand? As much as she wanted him, she couldn't bring herself to seduce him, a married man.

"Jeanile, what are you *talking* about?!?"

They stared at each other, angry and confused.

"You'd better start explaining from the top," he ordered tersely, oblivious to the fact that he was still butt naked and beautifully distracting.

Jeanile resisted the urge to tell him that the only way she could even begin to explain would be for him to put some clothes on. She bit her lips in agitation.

"I'm waiting." Ravenell defensively crossed his arms across his chest, waiting for her to begin.

Looking away from him, she decided to start on an offensive tack, for it was her best and only defense in this situation. "I saw you two together!" she blurted out.

"I'm sure you did for wherever we went Ramika was sure to follow," he said flippantly.

"No, I mean the night before our... our wedding!"

Ravenell blinked in confusion. He cocked his head to one side, staring at her incredulously. "Jeanile, you're not making any sense, honey." His voice was soft and hypnotic as he changed tactics to coax the story from her as if she were a child.

Jeanile resented his tone and she glared at him angrily. "Listen to me! I was *there*! I came to the hotel suite where you were supposed to have your bachelor party. I... I don't know what possessed me and I can't tell you how many times I regretted going there, but what can you do?" She shrugged nonchalantly, even though there was nothing nonchalant about her sordid, painful words. "As it is, you won't even bother to deny it!" she accused.

"Deny *what*? The only thing I've heard so far is that you think I'm married to Ramika! Which would be a pretty hard thing to be, considering she's already married to Steve."

"STEVE!?" Jeanile practically screeched his name.

"Yeah, Steve."

Jeanile frowned in confusion for a moment, but then her brow cleared when a solution popped into her mind. "Well, I guess you guys like to pass your women around, don't you?"

Ravenell moved as if to throttle the life from her but thought better of it. Instead, he turned his energy into collecting his clothes.

Jeanile watched him with dismay. She knew he was not what one would call a player and wished she could have recalled her statement. It was a low blow but the apology was stuck in the back of her throat.

"Well, are you going to finish this yarn or not?" he demanded after a few minutes of edgy silence and when he was fully clothed.

"I went to the hotel suite and was about to knock when I heard noises from inside." Her teeth worried her bottom lip with the painful memory. It seemed as if some wounds would never heal.

"And what, exactly, were these noises?" Ravenell asked patiently.

"You would know better than I would!" Jeanile shot back. "But from the sound of it, I think it's safe to say it was sex!"

Ravenell's face became a blank mask.

"Well…" Jeanile sighed, "At least I had the presence of mind to wait and have it out with you."

"But you *didn't* have it out with me!" Ravenell said loudly, the frustration of the situation straining his voice.

"No, I didn't. Instead, I waited and waited and then finally Ramika brought her sorry ass out the door." At this point Jeanile couldn't fight back the tears, and they began to pour freely down her cheeks. "I... I think that hurt more than anything else. That it should be a friend... an *intimate* friend... getting it on with my man."

Ravenell stared at her in shock. "So... that's why you left me at the altar," he accused, the pain of humiliation and lost years so evident in his voice.

Jeanile shrugged. "I hadn't planned to. Despite everything, I was pulled between marrying you or exposing you to a roomful of family members and friends. That's when I saw the tender look that Ramika sent you and I couldn't.... I couldn't go through with it." Jeanile sank on to the edge of the bed, defeated.

"You thought the worst of me, but still wanted to marry me? I guess in any other situation I would be flattered!"

"Whatever."

Jeanile was shivering at his calm tone. If he had railed at her and played the innocent by denying it, she would have felt somewhat better about the situation. Instead, she found his calm demeanor to be worrisome.

"Let's get something straight. I never cheated on you. Not once. Not with Ramika or anyone else for that matter. I had left the party early because I had had my fill of strippers and the boys were considering me a party pooper. Throughout the evening of drinking and titty flashing, all I could think about was you.

"I went straight to your apartment, but you weren't there. So I hung out there for as long as I could stand it and then I went home. I had left Steve in charge of the hotel suite, so I can only suppose that he was the one that you heard getting it on with Ramika."

"What?" It was Jeanile's turn to be shocked and amazed. "That can't be right... I mean..."

"Well, you guessed wrong. And as far as Ramika being married to me..." he shrugged his shoulders, at a loss as to how she could have possibly gotten her information incorrect.

"But the... the invitation..." Jeanile whispered helplessly.

"Did you read it?"

She shook her head helplessly.

"Well, if you *had* you would have seen that the blessed nuptials were for Ramika and *Steve*."

Jeanile looked away as warm tears filled her eyes.

"I should be angry, but I'm not. All I can think about right now are the painful weeks I spent in Puerto Rico, *alone*, trying to forget that that was supposed to be our honeymoon. Better yet all the months I waited for you to get over whatever hiccup you were going through and show up on my doorstep wearing my ring. Didn't you see that I said I would love you forever on that note I sent you? The one with the ring? Did you once think of the fact that you threw our love away?"

Jeanile could hold it in no longer. A huge wave of pain racked her body and the tears returned again in full force.

Ravenell went to her and gently put his arms around her as she cried. *What are we going to do?* he thought to himself as he held her in his arms rubbing her back in soothing circular motions.

He thought that the last few hours would have brought them closer together, but instead it had created an even greater rift between them – one so big that he suddenly wasn't sure if even love could heal it. He was confused, hurt and dismayed at the futility of the situation. For the past few years he had always imagined that simply holding her in his arms once again would be enough to reignite what they once had, to take a new step toward reconciliation once again. But now? Now he didn't know what to believe. The truth of the matter was she hadn't trusted him enough to believe in him when presented with circumstantial evidence. Instead, she had closed herself off and locked him out of her life - effectively killing any promise of a future they could have shared.

Ravenell felt helpless. He sincerely did love her, loved holding her in his arms again, but he didn't know how to get past the impossible situation she had placed them in. He needed time. To think - to try to clear his head. His gut twisted at the thought of leaving her like this. As far as he was concerned he had made every effort to reconcile and she had shot him down cold. He had put his job on hold just to be with her and he had had to beg her to give him a chance. He didn't think he could take another wave of rejection. *Why do I have to be the one to make all the effort? I'm sorry that things are the way they are but its not my fault!* He thought without a clear solution to the situation. He decided to delay things for the moment by just holding her in his arms.

"Oh, God!" she mumbled against his shirt. The despair and pointless years of pain she had caused them both pressed upon her heart further, threatening to break it in two.

"I... I think it's best if I leave now," Ravenell said as he gently brushed the tears from her cheeks. His heart couldn't stand it any longer. They were only causing each other greater pain, being together like this. He was a reminder to her of all she had given up by wrongly judging him, sentencing him falsely. And she? With her new confession, Ravenell suddenly realized that the pain and anguish he had felt the past four years was only growing stronger, just by looking at her again. Holding her. Again.

Jeanile gazed into his eyes, but shrunk back from the pity she saw in them. She guessed she must really be a pitiful creature in his eyes. "Yes," she whispered in defeat, "I understand."

Ravenell walked to the door, turning to give her a last look before silently slipping through the doorway and out of her life.

* * *

"*Now* what's the emergency?" Dominique asked Jeanile as she maneuvered her way through the airport traffic that typically clogged JFK International airport.

"Nothing. I just needed a ride. Jessica couldn't make it out today."

"That's right, you're back a day earlier than expected."

Jeanile shrugged. She had barely gotten through her speech at the convention and she had to admit that her speech was lackluster at best. She doubted that the few people who had attended paid much attention, however.

"You look awful, by the way." Dominique commented in her frank, no-nonsense way.

"I've been such a fool!" Jeanile blurted out and started to sob uncontrollably.

Dominique stared at her blankly for a moment, and then proceeded to cuss at the drivers that were blocking her exit from the airport. "I didn't mean you looked *that* bad, J..."

It was all Jeanile needed to produce some laughter—even if it was a bit strained.

"Well, that's a start, at least," Dominique said, merging over a lane. "Now, maybe you can tell me what the Beelzebub's Balls is going on?"

Jeanile took a deep breath and proceeded with her story. Dominique, for her part, uttered not a word, but instead listened intently, despite the fact that she was practically speeding down the highway.

"I tried to find him," Jeanile exclaimed as they got out of Dominique's car and made their way sans luggage to Dominique's apartment. She had spilled the whole story in the forty-five minutes it has taken them to get from the airport to the Dominique's front door.

"Hmm," was all Dominique had occasional said.

"I didn't know where he was staying and worse yet, I don't know what the hell I'm gonna do. I lost a good man! Out of stupidity and possibly insanity, and I... I know I wouldn't take me back if I were him."

"Well, I think you should stay here for the time being," Dominique offered.

"It's not like I'm homeless," Jeanile stated coolly.

"No. It's not that. I just don't think you should be alone right now. You have a lot of thinking to do, and I think you can best accomplish that in peace and quiet. If not here, then at least go to your parents."

"Dom, I can just see it now. 'Intelligent, confident sexual therapist slinks home to parents to lick her wounds.'"

Dominique rolled her eyes. "Whatever. Who ever said you were intelligent?" she said with a grin. Jeanile pushed her lightly. "Anyhow, it's just a suggestion. Take it or leave it. And while we're on the subject of suggestions, I think you should look Ramika up."

Jeanile's shoulders sagged. "Please, she wouldn't talk to me," she said, gratefully accepting the hot cocoa Dominique placed in her hand.

"You'd be surprised. Our group really hasn't been the same since you left us. But I wouldn't go telling her about the whole misunderstanding. Just say that you were going through a rough patch and needed to be by yourself for a little while—"

"Four years?" Jeanile commented dryly.

"Whatever. It's a stretch, but I bet Ramika would be so glad to see you that she'll treat everything like water under the bridge. Besides, she's so enraptured by her husband and new baby that you'll probably only get cooing noises from her." Dominique rolled her eyes in mock dismay. "Anyway, if anything else, it'll distract you for a little while, and that's just what the doctor ordered."

"I guess you're right."

"Of course I'm right!" Dominique quipped. "The Goddess... is never wrong."

Jeanile giggled and threw one of the ridiculously overstuffed cushions at her head.

Dominique ducked, sticking her tongue out on her way back to the kitchen.

Jeanile closed her eyes and thanked God for small blessings like sympathetic and compassionate friends.

* * *

"I already told you, Jeanile, he's out of town." Will's irritation was clearly apparent.

Jeanile gripped the receiver of her telephone in frustration. It seemed that Ravenell had fallen off the face of the earth. Soon after her visit to Ramika's, she was overcome by such a longing that she decided to swallow her pride and find him, to attempt a reconciliation. Unfortunately, the saying that 'a good man is hard to find' was becoming all too true. Ravenell had rented out his apartment and his taciturn agent refused to give her any information, other than he was unavailable.

"Fine," she fairly growled into the telephone.

"Good," Will stated flatly, and gave her a taste of the dial tone.

Jeanile glared at the telephone and knew that this was her last attempt to contact him. If he had gotten any of her messages he would have called, she reasoned. As it was, two months had come and gone and she was staring down the cold reality of the dreaded Christmas season.

She sighed. *Perhaps some things just weren't meant to be*, she thought. It was time to throw in the towel and move on.

*   *   *

Will stared morosely out of his office window as he mulled over what could be done about the Jeanile situation. This was beginning to escalate out of control. He knew that Ravenell still cared about her, but he also knew that Rav hadn't been the same since he had returned from Spain. He had driven himself into a frenzy to complete the job in Madrid, had returned stateside just long enough to put his apartment up for lease, packed his bags and had headed to the wilds of Africa.

Will turned his attention to the latest batch of negatives that Ravenell had sent him. There were pictures from the earthquake in Afghanistan, pictures of people rebuilding their lives after the devastation of the tsunami in India and, most recently, some very disturbing pictures of the status of civilian life in Iraq. It seemed like wherever there was danger, despair and devastation, Ravenell was there to capture it on film.

"What am I going to do with you?" Will asked the negative that he held up to the light for closer inspection.

His last, very brief conversation with Jeanile had revealed that whatever torture Ravenell was going through, she was experiencing it as well.

"Obviously, they can't live without each other," he mused as he gazed balefully at the telephone. "Maybe I should have told Rav about her calls." He stared down at his desk for a few seconds, collecting his thoughts.

"Anne, can you get Ravenell Wylde on the phone for me?" he shouted to his assistant over the intercom.

"Sure, if he's staying at the same place he was two days ago, but he's been moving around a lot," Anne complained.

"Just do your best. Thanks."

Will got up and paced the length of his office agitatedly as he waited for Anne to buzz him with the call.

"I could always just give her the last known number for him and let them duke out, but then, maybe Rav doesn't even want to talk to her. Yeah, I'd better okay it with him, first. He's been through so much because of that woman." Will muttered to himself as he paced up and down the room.

"Will, I've got Ravenell on the line for you," Anne called to him over the intercom.

Will practically raced back to his desk to get to the telephone. "Okay, put it through," he panted as he released the buzzer.

"Rav?" Will asked anxiously.

"Will?" Rav responded in a very sleepy, disoriented voice.

"Yeah."

"Do you have any idea what time it is?" he asked irritatedly as he focused his bleary eyes at the red dial of the hotel alarm clock.

"I don't even know where you are, so how could I possibly know the time?" Will fired back. He was tired of practically babysitting and then getting his head bitten off for trying to do the right thing.

"Well, for your information, it's four twenty in the morning and I'm in Istanbul."

"Well, bully for you. Look, I just wanted to tell you that the pictures you sent me were great, but I can't use them."

"What?!?"

Ravenell suddenly sounded wide awake and ready for a fight.

"They're good, very good but I just don't know if I have the market for them at the moment. Besides, I think it would be in your best interest to clean up your personal life first so that you won't send me these dark, depressing pictures."

"What do you mean?" It was practically a low, menacing growl.

"I mean, first you have to call Jeanile. She's been calling here incessantly."

There was complete silence at the other end.

"Rav?"

"Yeah, I'm here." Ravenell answered very slowly, almost as if he had been holding his breath.

"Don't worry. I told her that you're out of town. I've told her that several times a day. I would have *continued* telling her that, but I got your pictures and I think that whatever you guys are going through needs to be resolved. Now. *Before* you can get back to taking the kind of pictures I'm used to seeing!"

The silence was deafening.

"Are you still there?" Will asked. This was not the way he had expected Ravenell to take the news.

"Yeah."

"Look," Will said quietly, "I guess I can salvage some of the shots. I could probably get them to *National Geographic* or even the *Explorer*, but you have to come back so that I can fit you up with something more to your style, you know?" Will sounded as if he was pleading his case to a very biased jury.

"I'll think about it," Ravenell said.

"What about Jeanile?" Will asked anxiously.

"I'll think about that, too."

Will was left with the dial tone humming in his ears. He glared at the receiver and asked the gods above why he was saddled with some of the most difficult clients who would try even the patience of a saint.

DIEZ

Ravenell stamped his feet to get the life back into his toes, numb with cold from pacing the block where Jeanile's office was located the past half hour. He got the address from Steve two days ago, and now had finally worked up the nerve to actually use it.

As he walked through the lobby of her office building he couldn't help the swell of pride at seeing her progress as a professional. He smiled to himself as he signed in at the reception desk. He always knew she would eventually get what she desired, and they both knew early on that what she had truly wanted was an office on Park Avenue. He walked into the elevator and pressed the button for the eighth floor, then waited with mingled anticipation and dread as it steadily rose to come to a jarring halt at her floor.

The reception area was decorated in cool, neutral tones and there was nothing in the lighting or paintings on the wall to suggest it was a shrink's office. He smiled at the print of Monet's *Water Lilies* that hung behind the receptionist's desk. That was one of his favorites, and they had discussed it *ad nauseam* on one of the journeys to the Met.

"May I help you?" The receptionist asked politely as he approached her desk as casually as he could.

"Ah... yes, I'm here to see Jeanile Graham." Ravenell almost burst out laughing at the weird tone of his voice. It sounded meek and almost high-pitched, like a choir boy going through puberty.

The receptionist smiled encouragingly, prompting Ravenell to quickly attempt to explain that he wasn't a patient.

"That's alright," she informed him patiently. "Dr. Graham isn't in the office this week, but Dr. Penn is handling her cases until she returns. If you could just fill out these forms for me I'll see if he can see you today." She stood up and extended a clipboard of papers and a pen.

Ravenell held his hands up in protest. "No.. I mean... I'm sorry, there's been a slight misunderstanding. I'm not a prospective *patient* either. I'd really just like to speak to Jeanile, personally. But if that's not possible today, I could just leave her a message."

"Oh," the girl said, undaunted. She grabbed a note pad and a pen. "Okay, I can take your message."

Ravenell stared at her for a few seconds. "It's a *private* message," he finally said, calmly but firmly.

She blinked, and forced a smile. "Alright," She said as she handed him the pen, note pad and an envelope. After that she quickly returned her attention to her computer screen.

Ravenell eyed her suspiciously. *So much for the idea of a private message*, he thought. *She'll be on this the minute I walk out the door.* "On second thought, I think it can wait," he said, handing her everything back. Could you tell me when she'll be back in the office?"

"A week from today," came the crisp reply.

"Thank you."

Ravenell turned and walked back to the elevators. *Maybe it's for the best, Jeanile's not being here*, he thought. Some things simply couldn't be expressed effectively in a note.

*   *   *

Christmas had come and gone, and now Jeanile found herself staring down the empty tunnel of a New Year's Eve party at Dominique's. She had always liked parties — especially New Year's Eve parties. There was something exciting, clean and new about those nights of ushering out the old and welcoming the new. It was the promise of new beginnings, and forgiveness. Unfortunately, this was the first New Year's Eve she would celebrate since she made that horrible mistake of walking out on Ravenell.

This morning Dominique had called to remind her not to chicken out. Jeanile glared at her reflection in the mirror and decided that the red dress made her look too forlorn and depressed. She internally grimaced at the fact that the last time she wore red she had been enveloped in Ravenell's arms.

"Oh, Rav," she sighed as she shimmied out of the dress and tossed it onto the growing pile of discarded outfits, steadily evolving from a molehill into a mountain.

She had given up on ever reaching him, and on Dominique's advice went to her parents home for some much need soul searching, rest and relaxation during the Christmas Holiday week. It had been a balm to her soul. She had spent quality time with her sisters, Beth and Jessica, gotten "back to basics" with her mom in the kitchen, and shot the breeze with her dad in his makeshift study in the garage. It was nice to come home. It had distracted her from the sorry mess that was her love life.

But now she would have to face the music, showing up to a New Year's Eve party where all her old friends would be waiting. Friends that she had pushed out of her life the past few years. It was one thing to have a cozy, make-up lunch with Ramika and family. It would be quite another thing to walk into a party - *sans date* - to eat a heaping helping of humble pie.

Jeanile looked at the bedroom clock and frowned. She made a conscious effort to hurry and get dressed by picking up a random blouse to go with the black pants she had first tried on an hour ago. Applying some lipstick to her pouty, full lips, she blew her reflection a kiss and winked provocatively. "Here goes nothing," she whispered to herself.

Grabbing her coat, purse and scarf, she walked confidently out the door and into the snowy night.

*   *   *

Ravenell gazed anxiously at the white, gaily lit house with the big bold letters that proclaimed it was number 34. Elegant and well-decorated, the entire street exuded the contagious, festive spirit of its owners. Christmas had come and gone, but the colorful lights were still lit in honor of New Year's Eve. Though his body was growing cold from the wintry air, Ravenell continued to pace restlessly up and down the block. He had arrived half an hour earlier, and actually walked up the steps one time, only to lose his courage and turn back upon reaching the front door.

What would he say to her? How could he possibly convince her that they should try again? In his mind, he rehearsed an endless string of speeches in which he listed all the positive reasons why they shouldn't give up on a future together. In one scenario, he bared his heart and soul in an emotional plea, while in another he was completely rational, practical and—at least to him—entirely too robotic and lackluster. He closed his eyes and sighed. Somehow he needed to strike a tender balance between irrationally offering her all of his heart, body and soul—leaving none of his feelings hidden whatsoever—and maintaining a cool rationality behind the mask of control.

So here he was, stalking up and down the block, chilled and filled with the dread of being too vulnerable, too trusting. Doubting that they would ever make it back to where they could openly love and adore one another.

Ravenell stopped, took a deep, steadying breath and made his decision.

He would have to go in.

"It's now or never!" he said to himself.

Gritting his teeth, he walked up the steps, stood in front of the door and rang the doorbell to Dominique's apartment.

*   *   *

Jeanile had joined the party—already in full force—about four hours ago at the make shift bar. Someone had asked her to make a drink, and before she could blink an eye she had been securely ensconced behind the bar, handing out Harvey Wall Bangers, Woo Woos, Leg Spreaders and the always popular Sex-on-the-Beach. Deciding to make her presence felt on the dance floor, she kindly excused herself and sashayed to the cleared area of the apartment where everyone was moving in time to the beat. Unfortunately, she was just in time for the DJ, Uncle "JZ," to switch the music from hip hop to old skool. She knew what was coming next from past experience — old skool slow jams like Anita

Baker, Brian McKnight and Barry White. She rolled her eyes and smiled at Dominique, who threw her an apologetic grin in return.

Not having a partner, she gracefully and skillfully exited the dance floor. She had to admit, despite dreading the evening, she *was* having a good time. She had suppressed her butterflies and her nerves by having a few Rum and Cokes — just enough to get her nicely buzzed. The rest of her jitters had dissipated when she noticed that Ramika and Steve had come alone.

Glancing around the room, she noted that there were a lot of familiar faces. There was Auntie Val and Uncle Desi, Janice and Nicki, Lauren and her most recent Buju Banton look-a-like, Tracya and a few of her "new friends," B and her trainer boyfriend and a host of others. The room was full and buzzing with the excitement of ringing in the New Year. Jeanile took a sip of her Rum and Coke to cool down, and smiled at the antics that were taking place on the dance floor. She could sense the party was about to get rowdier, especially since it was about twenty-five minutes to midnight. She figured that this was as good a time as any to make her exit.

Making her way down the darkened hallway that led to Dominique's bedroom, she rehearsed some plausible excuses she could give to her host for sneaking out early. She giggled at the idea that she would need an excuse, and decided that if Dom gave her a hard time she would just tell her that the dog ate her homework. She turned on the bedroom light and began to rifle through the pile of coats on the bed, trying to locate hers.

"Leaving so soon?"

Jeanile's body froze at the sound of the voice. At first, happiness filled her heart, but disappointment quickly replaced it as logic convinced her of the impossibility. She probably imagined it. She sighed hopelessly, for she knew that Ravenell was miles - or perhaps half a world - away on assignment. Swiftly she resumed her task of locating her coat without even turning around.

Ravenell frowned in confusion and disappointment. He had noticed her paralysis at the sound of his voice, but was puzzled as to why she hadn't turned around. He waited uncertainly in the doorway, unsure if he should stay or go.

"Got it!" Jeanile exclaimed triumphantly as she grabbed her coat. She turned around to head back to the party to say her goodbyes. "Oh God!" It was a wail of despair as she realized that it wasn't her imagination after all and that she had completely ignored Ravenell for the past three minutes.

She rushed toward him in an effort to apologize, but stopped inches away. He looked rather irritable, and the thought that she had messed up—again—settled firmly into the pit of her stomach. She desperately wanted him to take her in his arms and hold her — giving her encouragement to pour her heart out to him.

His hesitation coupled with the displeased look on his face caused her to step back, once again sending him the wrong signal.

"I'm sorry. I didn't realize that... that..." Jeanile's voice sputtered into silence as her eyes drank in the beauty of him. *That what?* Her inner voice screamed. *That you thought he was a figment of your imagination? C'mon girl, get a life and fess up that you've been an idiot and that you would walk barefoot through the Sahara - or any other desert of his choosing - just to get a chance to make it up with him.*

"I—"

"Well—"

They both stopped short at the other's word.

"Go ahead," Ravenell nodded.

Jeanile smiled weakly — but it was still a smile. Ravenell returned her smile and stared at the beautiful woman in front of him. He felt as if his heart would burst through his ribs.

"How have you been?" He asked when she failed to start the conversation.

"Miserable," she answered simply with a nod. "And you?"

"Worse."

Jeanile smiled widely at the implication.

They shared the smile that broadened as they relaxed.

"I called your agency — a few times," she said hesitantly. She didn't think it was relevant to tell him that she had called everyday for a week.

"So I heard," Ravenell laughed. "I came as soon as I was able, and stopped by your office."

Jeanile frowned. "I didn't get a message."

Ravenell avoided her eyes and looked very uncomfortable. "I didn't leave a message."

"That was *you*? Denise thought you were a psych patient." She bit her lip to keep from laughing, unaware that her eyes were shining with merriment that lit up her face, her entire body language driving Ravenell to distraction.

"I miss you," he suddenly announced. Their eyes met in the recognition of their longing for each other's love, their companionship. That, and the lonely years they had wasted.

Jeanile swallowed the lump in her throat.

"I miss you," he continued, "and I ache for your presence in my life. I know we have a lot to work out, but I go to pieces without you. I don't want to just exist anymore — which is basically all I've been doing these past four years. I want to live again — really *enjoy* life. And... I can't do that without you." His words were simple, unabashed and sincere and he marveled at how easily the words flowed from his heart and poured from his lips. He looked away for a moment and back. "I.. don't *want* to do that... without you," he corrected.

Ravenell stepped closer to her, over the edge of safety. He didn't care about rejection anymore. He wanted her... *needed* her... and before this night was over she would know that. Then it would be up to her to walk away for good or take the first step in creating a lifetime of love with him.

"I want you in my life, in a home of our own, to cry with, laugh with, to love and trust and — everything. I want to go to bed with you every night and wake up with you every morning. I *love* you. And what I need to know is... what would it take to..."

Jeanile closed the gap between them and sealed his mouth with a gentle kiss. Ravenell sighed, melting into her softness as his lips opened in relief. Their kiss was a tender fulfillment and promise of their long-delayed joy, of finally finding completion. Of loving, and knowing that you were fully loved in return. Ravenell's arms encircled her waist, drawing her closer.

It was comforting, and Jeanile realized she wanted to be held like this for the rest of her life. "Rav, I love you," she whispered into his ear. He hugged her closer still at the sound of her delicious words.

"Say it again."

"*I love you, I love you, I love you!*"

A smile of contentment spread across his face and he kissed her on her forehead.

"And I love *that!*" Jeanile giggled. Her heart was light and she felt as if she could float away, but there was something she needed to say to clear the air. "Rav," she said as she looked down at her feet, "I'm so sorry. I... I wasted a lot of years because I doubted and misjudged you. When the truth came to light, I felt my heart breaking all over again. I'm truly sorry for all the pain I caused."

"Shhhhh….. That's all in the past. And now that I know that you're not suffering from commitment issues…"

"What?" Jeanile looked up at him with a puzzled look.

"Didn't I explain?"

"No." She shook her head in denial.

"When you left, I thought you were afraid to commit. I thought I had put too much pressure on you and that you were just scared and backed out. The fact that you didn't date anyone else the entire time only confirmed that."

"No, that wasn't it at all. I really just wanted to marry *you*."

"Then marry me now," Ravenell ordered with a tender smile.

"*Now?*" She sighed contently, snuggling closer to his chest to listen to his beating heart.

"Well, not this very minute, but I'm not going to wait for another big wedding. I don't care if I have to haul you off to Vegas and marry you in front of an Elvis impersonator. I want to marry you, Jeanile. As soon as possible."

Jeanile smiled at the thought and reached up to press kisses to every inch of his beloved face.

Ravenell held her in his arms tightly, reveling in the delight of holding his woman in his arms. His chest expanded with relief and wonder. The happiness coursed through his veins and filled him with a sense of undiluted, deep and abiding love.

"Five... four... three... two... one! Happy New Year!!!" The crowd in the living room shouted loudly, oblivious to the tender scene taking place in the bedroom.

Ravenell's lips descended onto hers once more, and their unspoken passion exploded between them like so many champagne bubbles.

Epilogue

Ravenell stood just outside the door to the nursery, a huge lime green frog with a red grin tucked under one arm and a huge Pooh bear stuffed under the other. He had silently crept up the staircase to surprise his beautiful wife and baby daughter. As he peeked around the corner, however, he soon realized that surprising them would be out of the question. Jeanile was sleeping soundly, curled up in the rocking chair with their tiny bundle of joy snuggled securely in her arms.

He tiptoed into the room, marveling once again at how quickly he had adjusted to the bright pink and orange décor of the nursery. He had thought Jeanile had lost her mind when she had chosen those colors, not to mention the impractical and ridiculous brass crib that had taken him ages to put together.

Of course, he was right. How else could they explain the frequent night runs to the store to buy outlandish concoctions in order to satisfy her intense cravings? For someone so intelligent and professional to suddenly crave pickles smothered with ketchup... it was enough to throw him for a loop. He liked to kid her about it, but deep down he knew she was worth it. Besides, he had been unable to deny her anything in the two years that they had been married.

The room looked nice and cozy, and he found himself ecstatic to be back. He crept closer and placed a tender kiss on her relaxed lips. Jeanile smiled and opened her tired eyes.

"You're back early!" she whispered as she stretched her free hand out to welcome him.

"Yeah. They've nicknamed me the 'speed demon' because I drive my team at high speed just so I can come back to my Wylde Honey."

Jeanile's smile deepened at the sound of her beloved nickname.

"We missed you, too."

Ravenell put the new toys down and stroked his daughter's soft, curly hair. It was a miracle that such a tiny little thing could twist his heart around her little fingers so tightly, and he gazed in wonder as Jana opened her eyes and smiled up at him in recognition.

Gently, he scooped her up from her mother's arms and began to coo at her.

Jeanile looked at the huge frog and Pooh bear and shook her head. She wondered where she was going to put them in the well-stocked nursery.

"You are going to spoil her," she said in mock disappointment.

"How can I spoil the next president of the United States? Hmmm?" He continued with his cooing noises, eliciting giggles and wriggles of delight from his daughter.

"Yeah, *woo woo wooo*. How can I spoil my darling? Koochie, koochie. Should we tell mommy that we got something for her, too? Should we tell her that it's in my left pants pocket?" He flashed a grin at Jeanile as he danced up and down the room, gently rocking Jana in his arms.

Jeanile strolled up to him and stroked his hair, face and neck. "I would rather a kiss instead," she whispered laughingly.

Ravenell leaned down carefully and placed a long, lingering kiss on her waiting lips. "It's good to be home," he said. He kissed her on the forehead and drew her close against his heart, knowing that now, after so many years, their love was more secure than ever.

About the Author

As a longtime reader of romance novels and a respected critic of contemporary, multicultural romance novels for the *Romantic Times Magazine*, Shamaine recently decided it was time to transition into the role of a writer. After extensive amounts of research, she soon realized that making the shift from avid reader to published author can be extremely difficult. Difficult, but not impossible. Thus, with the publication and success of her first novel, *This Burning Desire*, Shamaine soon began to take the first of many steps in establishing herself as a leading romance novelist.

Raised in New York by way of Jamaica in the West Indies, Shamaine is gifted with the ability to tell a story with creativity and flair. Readers will crave the flavor of the Caribbean Islands mixed with a healthy dash of New York chutzpah. Shamaine uses her heritage, personal experiences and vivid imagination to create a cast of interesting and intriguing characters that will capture the interests of even the most passionate romance reader.

Wylde Honey is Shamaine's second novel, and she hopes that readers will enjoy reading it as much as she enjoyed writing it. She is currently employed at a major Park Avenue law firm and is hard at work completing her third novel, *Confessions of a New York Nympho*.

New College Nottingham
Learning Centres

CPSIA information can be obtained at www.ICGtesting.com
Printed in the USA
LVOW081535040213

318566LV00003B/489/A

9 781412 083713